FY P

book
ng t

CW00496364

'I didn't want to give anyone the wrong impression.'

'Aren't you afraid *I'll* get the wrong idea?'

'No.' Clare turned to face him and met his gaze unblinkingly. 'You have the same problem—because you look the way you do, no one will take you seriously. I know you understand,' she told him frankly.

'That doesn't make me immune to your charms,' Michael said softly.

Dear Reader

Caroline Anderson's PERFECT HERO has a shock in store, while Dr Laura Haley is determined to pull Dr Ben Durell out of his refuge in Marion Lennox's THE HEALING HEART. We welcome back Sonia Deane, who tackles the thorny question of doctor/patient integrity, while TOMORROW IS ANOTHER DAY by Hazel Fisher explores the recovery of two people who have been badly hurt in the past. Enjoy!

The Editor

Caroline Anderson's nursing career was brought to an abrupt halt by a back injury, but her interest in medicine led her to work first as a medical secretary, and then, after completing her teacher training, as a lecturer in medical office practice to trainee medical secretaries. In addition to writing, she also runs her own business from her home in rural Suffolk, where she lives with her husband, two daughters, mother and dog.

Recent titles by the same author:

A GENTLE GIANT
MORE THAN TIME

A PERFECT HERO

BY

CAROLINE ANDERSON

MILLS & BOON LIMITED
ETON HOUSE   18–24 PARADISE ROAD
RICHMOND   SURREY   TW9 1SR

My grateful thanks to the following people for
their help:

Jeff and Maggie Hallett
Charlie McLaren and all at Shotley Point Marina
Peter Graves and Sunbeam, for Henrietta

*First published in Great Britain 1992
by Mills & Boon Limited*

© Caroline Anderson 1992

Australian copyright 1992

ISBN 0 263 13349 4

*Set in 10 on 12 pt Linotron Times
15-9208-52717*

*Typeset in Great Britain by Centracet, Cambridge
Made and printed in Great Britain*

CHAPTER ONE

'THOSE boys are the pits!'

Half laughing, half furious, Clare pushed the door of Sister's office shut behind her and sagged into the chair.

'That bad?'

Her head jerked up, her eyes instantly caught and trapped by a gaze so vivid she thought she must be dreaming. He was fair, his sun-streaked hair falling in defiant strands across the bronze skin of his high forehead, and he radiated health and energy. He was also drop-dead good-looking, and Clare was instantly wary.

'I'm sorry—I didn't realise there was anyone in here—not that I usually talk to myself, but this morning. . .!'

'Losing your grip already?' His voice was like rich silk sliding over pebbles. The stranger glanced at his watch and raised an eyebrow. 'It's only ten past nine!'

'Yes, well, if you'd met Danny Drew and his gang of fellow-sufferers, you'd understand!'

'I shall look forward to the experience.' He took a long, lazy stride forward and held out his hand across the desk. 'We haven't met. Michael Barrington. I'm Tim Mayhew's senior reg., as of about ten minutes ago. And you're Clare Stevens,' he added, engulfing her hand in his long, lean fingers.

A tingle like an electric shock ran up her arm, and she hastily detached herself from his hand and

5

smoothed her dress over her hips in an unconsciously provocative gesture.

'How did you know?' she asked, still rattled by the contact, and his hand reached out and flicked the badge on her breast pocket with casual disregard for convention.

'Oh—how silly of me!' She tried to smile, but her lips felt stiff and uncooperative. Those shatteringly blue eyes were inches from her own, and he was clearly laughing at her. She stood up breathlessly and turned away, to put some distance between herself and this young Adonis who had dropped out of the sky into her life. 'We were expecting you—I'm afraid Sister O'Brien's got the morning off—she's on from twelve-thirty. Would you like me to show you the ward?'

He nodded. 'Just informally—I don't want pomp and ceremony and a great trailing entourage!'

She laughed, an easy, rippling sound, and relaxed. 'We don't tend to stand on ceremony at the Audley Memorial. We'd better get on—we're not on take today, but we've got some elective patients in for hip replacement and it was one of those fairly bloody weekends on the road—we've got two lads in ITU who'll be coming up shortly if they're sufficiently stable.'

'I get your drift,' he said with a smile, and her heart crashed against her ribs. 'Allow me——'

He reached round her and opened the door, and as he did so she became aware of his height, and breadth, and the smooth skin of his jaw slightly roughened by stubble. Mingled with the faint scent of expensive cologne was a deeper, more intrinsic scent, primitive and masculine, that made her breath catch in her throat.

Thanking him in what she hoped was a normal voice,

she preceded him through the door and took him round the ward, showing him the utility areas and general geography before taking him round the four six-bedded bays and telling him about the patients who would be under his care.

'Do you want to examine any of them?' she asked as they went into the first bay.

'No, I don't think there's any need—unless there's anybody you feel I should look at in particular? I'm really only here to familiarise myself with the ward. I'll be joining Mr Mayhew in Theatre later.'

As they walked round the ward, Clare became increasingly conscious of her companion. He smiled and joked and stole the hearts of all the elderly ladies with their hip replacements, and he listened intently as she explained about their treatment of young Tina White, thrown from her horse and suffering from severe bruising of the spinal cord following a fracture dislocation of T4 and T5. She was being nursed on a revolving Stryker bed, and was turned every two hours throughout the day and night.

'She's a model patient, aren't you, Tina?' Clare said with a smile.

The girl grinned. 'Anyone's a model patient compared with that lot!' She waved her hand towards the end bay.

Clare groaned. 'The trouble is, they aren't in enough pain any more!'

Beside her, Michael Barrington frowned. 'You surely wouldn't want them to be in pain?' he said reprovingly.

'Of course not,' she laughed. 'Just well and back home again!'

Tina chuckled. 'They aren't so bad, really—takes

the edge off lying here day after day. At least I can try
and guess what they'll get up to next!'

'Any sign of improvement?' he asked quietly as they
walked away.

'Not really. We were very hopeful at first, but in fact
it looks pretty grim for her still. I'll fill you in in a
minute.'

They entered the last bay, and ducked to miss a
flying grape.

'Danny Drew?' he said wryly, and she laughed.

'Well, Mr Barrington, how did you guess?' She
picked up the fallen grape and turned her back on
Danny. 'He's fractured both femurs, so he's totally
immobilised. He's not an ideal patient by any stretch
of the imagination! Mr Mayhew fixed them both inter-
nally to make his management easier, but frankly I
think he would have had to wire his jaw to make any
appreciable differences——'

'Hello, darlin'! Brought the boyfriend, have you?'

There was a chorus of cat-calls which she ignored,
and beside her the SR chuckled under his breath. 'I see
what you mean! Right little joker, isn't he?'

She rolled her eyes and continued, 'That lad over
there, in the corner—Pete Sawyer—he came off his
bike and smashed his wrist and forearm, broke his
pelvis and did his patella a certain amount of no good.
Unfortunately his arm isn't fusing very well—he'll
probably have to go back to Theatre and have it
repinned. Otherwise they're all progressing nicely and
should be out in a short while.'

'You don't sound as glad as I'd imagine you'd be,'
he said as they made their way back to Sister's office.

She laughed. 'Why should I be glad? There'll be
another lot the same—we save that bay for the bikers

and the sports injuries. It's referred to fondly as Borstal.'

He chuckled. 'I can see why.' He eased his long frame into a chair and stretched out his legs. 'Tell me about Tina.'

'Sure. Coffee?' She poured two cups, set them down on the desk and flicked open the Kardex. 'Fell from her horse last Saturday—nine days ago. She was at a gymkhana and her horse shied and dropped her across a post and rail fence. She landed on her back. The spinal cord isn't severed, but there was extensive bruising and pressure from the dislocation. That's reduced with time, and Mr Mayhew's still hoping for some return of function, but so far it doesn't look hopeful. He may try and stabilise her further with surgery if she doesn't show any improvement, so we can get her rehabilitation under way sooner. In the meantime, we keep her turning and hope for a miracle.'

'Unlikely.'

'I know.' She stirred her coffee idly. 'Pete Sawyer is a problem, as well, with his unstable forearm fractures. I think Mr Mayhew is concerned he may end up with a non-union of the radius and ulna. They were very badly shattered.'

'How long ago?'

'Six weeks—plenty of time for a callus to form, but there's no sign of any regeneration.'

'Got the X-rays?'

'Mmm, they're with the notes.'

She found them and put them on the light-box, and they stood side by side examining them.

'What a bloody awful mess! He was lucky not to lose his arm.'

'Fortunately the soft-tissue injuries weren't too

extensive, otherwise I think Mr Mayhew might have been tempted to amputate.'

'That would be a shame.'

'It would be a tragedy in such a young man.'

He gave a short laugh. 'Amputation is always a tragedy, but the injury or disease giving rise to it is just as much of a problem. Often patients are better off without the traumatised limb.'

She shuddered. 'I can't believe that. Surely anything is better than losing a limb?'

'Oh, come on! I'll grant you a functioning limb, especially an arm, with even limited function can be more use than an artificial limb, but a neat amputation at a carefully chosen site and a properly fitting prosthesis in a well-adjusted patient causes far less change in lifestyle and social habits than a disablingly damaged limb—and it can be a lot less unsightly!'

'And what about the emotional aspects?' she asked heatedly. 'What about the effect on family? The personal problems, sexual problems and so on?'

'Hey, hey. . .' His hand came up and his knuckles brushed her cheek lightly, tantalisingly. 'Don't get so het up. Of course there are problems. Amputees need a lot of support and therapy, but all I'm saying is, with the right support, under certain circumstances they can be better off!'

She wanted to argue, but the brush of his knuckles was doing strange things to her circulation and her brain felt fogged. He was too close, too male, too— just too much! Their eyes were locked, his so intense she could almost feel their heat.

'Mr Barrington——'

'Michael.'

'Michael, then. Please stop. I can't think.'

'Good. I get the feeling that if you think, you'll start arguing with me again, and that would be a shame.'

She was sure he was going to kiss her. His firm, well-sculptured lips were inches from her own, and closing fast. . .

The shrilling of the phone was shattering. Clare leapt as if she'd been burned, and snatched up the receiver breathlessly.

'For you,' she muttered, handing him the instrument and backing away behind the desk. What on earth was wrong with her? For years she had been pursued by an endless stream of handsome and not-so-handsome young doctors, all convinced that with her looks she was a sexy little airhead who would be more than content to convey her favours on them. They had all been disappointed, but none more so than Clare herself, who had longed for years to be wanted for herself! Not for her body, or her face, but for her mind, her sense of humour, her zest for life.

Perhaps it had been easy to keep them at a distance, because universally and to a man they had failed to reach that elemental core of spirit that made her a woman. But this man—one brush of his hand, and her legs felt on the point of collapse, her blood-pressure had sky-rocketed and her body was thrumming with wild and primitive passion! You're pathetic, she told herself disgustedly.

He replaced the receiver and turned to her with a smile. 'The gods have spoken—I have to go up to Theatre and prove myself under the eagle eye of the boss. Are you doing anything later?'

'Washing my hair,' she replied promptly.

'Liar,' he said with a soft laugh. 'Come and have something to eat with me and tell me all I need to know about the hierarchy of this establishment. I'd hate to put my foot in it for the sake of a little friendly advice!'

She was tempted—oh, so tempted. As she hesitated, he watched her with a slightly quizzical expression, his vivid blue eyes seeming to see straight through her.

'Is there a reason for your procrastination?'

'Do I need a reason?' she retorted, almost crossly.

'No. I just wondered if you had a Significant Other.'

'A significant what?'

'Other—you know, husband, fiancé, boyfriend, live-in-lover—whatever.'

She shook her head. 'No—no whatever whatsoever.'

He frowned in mock disbelief. 'Really? No current lover?'

'No lover at all—full stop—nor am I looking for one!'

'What a tragic waste.'

'You think so? I'm quite content——'

'Content?' he snorted. 'Damn, Clare, a woman as beautiful as you should be more than content——'

She fixed him with a withering look. 'If you're offering to relieve my sexual frustration, Mr Barrington, you can save yourself the trouble. The answer's no!'

He threw back his head and laughed, a rich, warm laugh that rolled round her senses and left her feeling even more disorientated. Then he sobered slightly, and shot her a disarming grin. 'It's usual to wait until you're asked, isn't it? As a matter of fact, I wasn't offering—yet. Although, to be fair, I might well have got round to it——'

'You all do, some more quickly than others, but in the end you all make the same moves,' she said with a touch of bitterness, 'and the answer's always the same. Thanks, but no, thanks. Hadn't you better go?'

'Yes, I must. I'll see you later, Clare. Thanks for the ward-round and the coffee.'

And he was gone, leaving her feeling fraught with conflicting emotions. What a way for their professional relationship to get off the ground! Dear God, perhaps she had over-reacted, but there was no mistaking his interest. At twenty-five, Clare was something of an expert at interpreting masculine appraisal, and she was seldom mistaken.

And that man was interested.

Well, he'd soon discover that she wasn't that sort of girl, and, with his looks, if all he wanted was a little recreation he would soon be overrun with offers.

Sighing a little and not understanding quite why, Clare left the office and went about her duties.

Her peace was short-lived. He was back at one with Mr Mayhew, the orthopaedic consultant, and David Blake, the junior registrar, and he looked even better than her fevered mind had remembered.

Sister O'Brien fell instantly under his spell, the motherly woman welcoming him to the ward like the prodigal son, and Clare watched in helpless fascination as he examined the two patients whose hip replacements he had performed that morning.

'Good. That looks fine,' he said with a smile, covering up the second patient, and turning to Clare to hand her the notes. 'Thank you, Staff,' he said, then, lowering his voice, he added, 'What are you doing after you wash your hair?'

Ripping it out in handfuls, she thought, and choked down the laugh. 'Nothing,' she admitted quietly.

'Then come with me. Just a simple meal—nothing elaborate. Take pity on a stranger, Clare. I don't know a soul—doesn't it worry you that I'll be going home to a strange house all alone tonight, and every night? No one to talk to, to share anything with, except my cat, and his conversational skills are strictly limited. Please?'

'All right,' she relented with a laugh. 'When and where?'

'Do you live in the hospital?'

She nodded.

'Main entrance, seven o'clock? I'll pick you up.'

'OK. What shall I wear?'

'Anything—jeans? They do good food in the village pub, and we can sit in the garden. Must go. I'll see you at seven.'

As he turned, she was conscious of Sister O'Brien's interested scrutiny. They walked back to her office in silence, and for a moment Clare thought she'd got away with it. She was wrong.

'Nice young man. You seemed to hit it off very well with him, Clare.'

'He asked me to spare him some time this evening to tell him about the hospital—routine, things he ought to know, et cetera—you know how it is when you start somewhere new,' she said, modifying the truth for the sake of convention. Not for the world would she reveal how her heart had soared and spun out of control as he had handed back the notes and his hand had deliberately brushed against hers.

Sister O'Brien smiled to herself. About time, she thought. 'You'll enjoy it, dear—do you good to get out. Now, about Pete Sawyer—I believe Mr Mayhew wants Mr Barrington to have a go at refixing that wrist—I think they're going to try a bone graft now his pelvis is nearly healed and they can take bone from the ilium. Perhaps that'll do the trick.'

Just so long as he doesn't amputate for the hell of it, she thought to herself as she recalled their earlier conversation.

The day dragged. Not even to herself would Clare admit the reason, but as she went off-duty and found herself rummaging through her wardrobe for an appropriate alternative to jeans for a pub snack, she was brought up sharply against the realisation that her tingling sense of anticipation had only one cause—and that cause was Michael Barrington.

'Damn!' she muttered to herself, and all through her shower and preparation for the evening, she worried about her reaction to him. Because he was quite evidently a womaniser, and she had no intention of surrendering her hard-fought scruples to some trifling playboy just because he made her senses reel!

Her preparations complete, she stood in front of the wardrobe mirror and studied her reflection. Her blonde hair, released form the starched white cap and freshly washed, tumbled in casual layers to brush her collar lightly at the back. Her make-up, slightly heavier than usual, was still restricted to a smudge of soft grey-green shadow over her wide almond-shaped eyes, a touch of soft pink lipstick and the lightest feathering of mascara to tint the pale tips of her lashes. Casual, he had said, so she was wearing a soft cotton sweater the same grey-green as her eyes, and a pair of culottes in a rust and green print. Her legs were bare, her feet comfortably shod in soft cotton canvas slip-ons. She wondered if the whole effect was too casual, but it was too late to worry.

At five to seven, her heart pounding, she let herself out of her flat and made her way down to the main entrance of the hospital.

As she emerged on to the steps she saw Michael in the staff car park, deep in conversation with two of the consultants. She hung back, not quite ready yet to have her name publicly connected to his, but he had seen her and, making his excuses, he strode quickly towards her, a smile on his lips.

'Clare—you're on time!'

'What did you expect?'

He laughed. 'I expected you to be like most girls—late!'

'I'm not most girls,' she said repressively, and he laughed again.

'So I'm beginning to realise. Come on, I'm starving.' He took her arm and led her towards the car park. 'Oh, I have a confession—I rang the pub, and they don't do food on a Monday night, so before I spring it on you I wondered if you would consider allowing me to cook for you.'

Her heart sank. Here we go, she thought, and she slowed to a halt.

'In your house?'

'My cottage. You needn't worry, I'm a good cook, but apart from the local pub I haven't found anywhere else yet in the few days since I moved—by all means suggest something else if you'd rather, but I can promise you I have no intention of jumping your bones, my love.'

She gave a surprised little laugh, and glanced up at him. 'Am I so transparent?'

He grinned. 'You were as jumpy as a cat this morning, so it wasn't hard to put two and two together. I promise to keep my hands to myself if you do.'

'If I do? What do you mean?' she squeaked.

He gave a wry little laugh. 'You think you're the only one who gets treated like a sex object? Believe me, it makes a refreshing change to meet someone who isn't all over me like a rash after fifteen seconds!'

Well, and who could blame them? Clare thought to herself, recognising the slight bitterness behind the apparently arrogant remark. If she wasn't so busy saying no all the time she might well be tempted herself! She smiled at him. 'You've got a deal. You cook, I'll talk, and we can both clear up afterwards. How's that?'

'Great. Here we are. Hop in.'

He opened the door of a sleek red beastie, and she was instantly glad she hadn't worn a mini-skirt.

'Wow!'

He grinned self-consciously as he settled himself beside her behind the wheel. 'It's my brother's. I have a battered old Volvo estate for dragging all the boat stuff around, but he's in Germany for four months on business and suggested I borrow it to bolster the image!'

She laughed. 'It works! What is it?'

'A Porsche. Do you want the hood down?'

'Why not? It won't do my image any harm either!'

They laughed together, and with the touch of a button the hood folded down behind them and the June evening flooded in.

'Let's go, then!'

With a subtle roar, the engine leapt into life and they

coasted smoothly out of the car park. Clare settled back into the soft leather seat and sighed contentedly.

When they were on the open road he unleashed the power a little and soon the wind was whipping her hair round her face and bringing the colour to her cheeks. She laughed in delight. 'Michael, this is fabulous!'

'Good, isn't it? Lucky devil. I wonder if he'll sell it to me?'

He threw her a cheeky grin, and then turned his attention back to the road. After a little while they turned off the main road and headed along a winding lane, leading eventually to another lane and thence a rutted track.

'Where are we going?' Clare asked, suddenly conscious of their isolation.

He pointed. 'Over there—that little pink cottage.'

'Goodness, it is in the wilds of nowhere!' Clare said as they pulled up outside the cottage. It was tiny, the thatch low down on the walls arching like eyebrows over the little upstairs windows. The warm pink of the faded terracotta walls blended with the soft apricot of a climbing rose that tumbled in profusion over the front door, and more roses clustered under the little latticed windows.

'Don't tell me—it's called Rose Cottage!'

He chuckled. 'How did you guess? Come on in. Welcome to my humble abode.'

He doffed an imaginary cap and flung open the door with a flourish.

Inside it was just as charming, heavily beamed as she might have expected from a Suffolk cottage, with fascinating little nooks and crannies, and the furniture was mostly old pine. There was a Suffolk brick floor in the kitchen, and the steep staircase was tucked in under the eaves.

'Oh, Michael, it's lovely!'

He grinned. 'Thank you. You're my first visitor—let me show you round.'

She followed him, enchanted, as he climbed the steep stairs.

'Mind your head,' he said as he led her on to the little landing. 'It wasn't built for people as tall as us, I don't think.' He waved his arm. 'Bathroom here, and a bedroom at each end—neither of them exactly furnished to excess at the moment, but I'll get there. I only took possession of it last Thursday—I should have had it early in the week but I got caught in a storm off the Scillies.'

'The Scillies? The islands, you mean?'

He nodded. 'Yes—I took *Henrietta* out there for a few days' R and R, and it backfired on me a bit.'

Heavens, she thought, here we are, standing in the middle of his bedroom and he's telling me all about his problems with Henrietta, whoever she is!

'I'll take you to see her some time—she's very pretty, and I can handle her on my own easily unless the wind's very fierce. She's a bit of a handful then. You'll like her—do you get seasick?'

It dawned on Clare that *Henrietta* must be his boat, and she almost laughed out loud—till she realised that the feeling she had experienced had probably been jealousy. She wasn't sure, she'd never felt it before, and couldn't imagine for the life of her why she was feeling it now, but life was full of little surprises. . .

'No, I don't get seasick—or I didn't. I haven't sailed since I was about thirteen, but I used to go out a lot with my brother before that.'

'Snap! We had a Mirror, then a Fireball. *Henrietta* was my grandfather's boat—I spent a lot of time on her with him when I were a lad, as they say.'

Their laughing eyes met, and Clare was suddenly terribly conscious of the high iron and brass bedstead behind them.

'Why don't you go on down and find yourself a drink? There's white wine in the fridge, or red if you prefer, open on the side, and all sorts of soft drinks—I just want to get out of this suit and relax a bit.'

'Fine,' she said, a trifle breathlessly, and turned for the stairs as he stripped off his tie and kicked off his shoes. She heard them land with a thud as she ran down the stairs, and then he was humming, and she could hear drawers opening and shutting above her head as she rummaged in the kitchen for the fridge. She was still looking for it when he ran lightly down the stairs in his bare feet, clad only in a pair of old jeans that clung lovingly to every contour of his body. He was tugging on a T-shirt over his head, and his chest gleamed golden brown under the soft scatter of blond curls.

Her fingers itched to touch him, and she rammed her hands into her pockets to control them.

'Where's the fridge?' she asked, her voice sounding strained to her ears.

'Here—sorry!' He opened a cupboard like all the others, hand-built in dark oak to match the beams, and she saw a built-in fridge tucked in behind the door.

'How clever!'

'It's been well done—it belonged to an interior designer who's gone to Scotland to escape the rat race.'

'Rat race—here?'

He laughed. 'Over-populated, she said. I gather their

nearest neighbour up there is ten miles away. Red, white or something soft?'

'White with something in it?'

'Good idea.' He took a bottle of hock from the fridge, pulled the cork deftly and splashed it into two tall glasses, adding soda water and ice.

'Cheers!'

'Cheers! Welcome to the Audley.'

He smiled. 'Thank you, Clare. Right, sit down over there and tell me all the pitfalls—who's fallen out with who, who I mustn't speak to, who does the crossword in the staff lounge, all that sort of thing.'

It was her turn to laugh. 'Nothing like that. The Audley's a very happy hospital, and there's practically no hierarchy. We're all in the same business, after all.'

'Well, thank God for that! My last hospital was the giddy limit—I was forever treading on someone's toes.' He put the washed lettuce in the salad spinner, and placed it on the table in front of her. 'Now, what do you fancy? I've got a fresh sea-bass, or we could have steak if you'd prefer.'

'Did you catch the bass?'

He laughed. 'Afraid not, not this time. I bought it from the guy on the next boat. He caught it last night.'

'Sounds wonderful.'

While she spun the lettuce and made the salad, he washed the fish, stuffed it with butter and a handful of fresh fennel from the garden, and pinned it together with cocktail sticks.

'Thirty minutes in the oven,' he said with a grin. 'Time for a walk round the garden.'

It was lovely, heavy with scent and ripe with colour, and in the last rays of the June sunshine it was quite intoxicating.

Michael's enthusiasm was infectious, as he discovered things in the garden and pointed out others to her that he had noticed before. Under a tree at the end was a swing, old and creaky, but he tested it and then offered her a ride.

She shook her head. 'I never could make them go high enough.'

The next second his arm had snagged her waist and she was on his lap, swinging high in the air and laughing with delight as the wind tugged at her hair and the ground rushed up to meet them.

Finally he slowed it, and as they drifted gently back and forth, his lips touched warmly against hers before his arm released her.

She stood up, her legs shaking, but whether from the dizzying ride or the effects of the kiss she wasn't sure. After all, it had only been a very tiny kiss, not at all the sort of thing that smouldering passion was made of, but it had affected her more deeply than she dared admit, even to herself. She could still feel the hard imprint of his thighs against her legs, and the warmth of his chest against her side.

'The fish,' he said abruptly, and she followed him back to the kitchen, her emotions in turmoil. As he unwrapped the bass and lifted it carefully on to the plate, she forced herself to behave calmly.

'Do you have any salad dressing?'

'In the little jar in the fridge door—it's home-made.'

They sat at the big oak table in the kitchen for their meal, and to her surprise she relaxed and enjoyed it. The food was delicious, Michael friendly but nothing more, and she began to think she must have imagined her reaction to his kiss.

They took their coffee in the garden and sat on the

bench seat among the roses, he at one end, she at the other, and a respectable distance between them. After a while their conversation flagged, and she looked up to see him watching her, his eyes intent.

She flushed. Perhaps she hadn't imagined it? His arm was flung along the back of the seat, and his fingers reached out and brushed the side of her neck. Her pulse leapt to life, and she sprang to her feet.

'I ought to go, Michael.'

He stood up smoothly and reached for her hand, his thumb idly brushing against her wrist.

'I can feel your pulse,' he murmured. 'It's racing. Fight or flight, or something even more fundamental?'

She was frozen, transfixed to the spot, as he closed the gap between them and cupped her face gently in his hands.

'Have I told you how lovely you look tonight?'

'I—no, I don't think so. . .'

'How remiss of me. You're beautiful, Clare. Quite exquisite.' Trapped in that paralysing blue gaze, she was powerless to move as he lowered his head and took her mouth in a kiss so gentle, so delicate that she thought she must be dreaming.

She sighed softly, and he eased her closer, so close that she could feel the beating of his heart against her own. Her lips parted slightly, and he deepened the kiss, his tongue tracing the edge of her teeth.

'Open your mouth,' he murmured gruffly against her lips, and she obeyed mindlessly, oblivious to everything except the feel of his body against hers, the touch of his hands on her face, the devastating intimacy of his kiss.

With a muffled groan he lifted his head and rested his cheek against her hair. She could feel the thudding of his heart, the slight tremor in his muscles as he held her close against his chest.

'I think I'd better take you home now,' he said after a moment, and she nodded speechlessly.

Neither of them spoke on the journey back to the hospital, but as he turned to leave her at her door, she laid a hand on his arm.

'Thank you for a lovely evening, Michael,' she said softly.

'The pleasure was all mine,' he murmured.

Clare smiled and shook her head. 'Not all of it,' she replied gently, and, rising on to her toes, she kissed his cheek lightly. 'Goodnight.'

'Goodnight, Clare. See you tomorrow.'

And she would, she thought with a little race of her heart. For the first time in a long, long while, she found herself looking forward to seeing a man again. The smile was still on her lips as she fell asleep.

CHAPTER TWO

IT WAS a busy week, and one in which Clare saw frustratingly little of Michael, and that only in brief snatches on the ward.

Two of the boys in 'Borstal' went home, to be replaced by one of the lads from ITU—the other had been moved direct to Stoke Mandeville—and another admission, a youth of seventeen who had come off his motorbike and fractured his femur.

He was in traction with a Steinmann pin and was comfortable enough to join in with the general hilarity after twenty-four hours.

Pete Sawyer had had a bone graft taken from his hip and placed in his arm to link the broken ends of his radius, and they were now hoping for some progress.

Tina, on the other hand, showed no progress, and on Thursday Mr Mayhew discussed with her the possibility of fusing her spine so they could start the long process of her rehabilitation.

She was stoical throughout, but Clare sensed her outward calm was just a front. Her mother, however, had no such outward calm, and on Friday Clare had to remove her from Tina's bedside because she had collapsed in tears.

She took Mrs White into the office and met Michael there, studying case notes. He had been in on the dicussion with Tim Mayhew and the Whites, and the decision-making beforehand, and Clare gratefully

25

handed the distressed woman over to him while she
went back to see Tina.

The girl had tears in her eyes, the first real tears
Clare had seen, and in a way she was relieved. She
drew the curtains quietly round and sat beside her,
holding her hand.

'I don't want to be in a wheelchair for the rest of my
life,' she whispered, and then the great heavy tears
came, running down her wan cheeks and trailing into
her hair.

There was nothing constructive to say, so Clare held
her hand, and gradually the sobs subsided, leaving her
weary and shaken.

'I don't think I can face my mum again for a while,'
she told Clare, and she nodded.

'I'll suggest she goes and has a look round the shops
and comes back later, shall I?'

Tina shot her a grateful look. 'Would you? I just
can't deal with her as well.'

Clare squeezed her hand and went back to the office.

'How is she? I didn't mean to upset her, but she's
only seventeen—too young for all this——' Mrs White
buried her face in her hands and sobbed again.

Over her head Clare met Michael's eyes. He jerked
his head towards the door, and Clare nodded.

'Mrs White, I'll get you a cup of coffee. You stay
here for a minute and I'll be back.'

She followed Michael out and up to the ward
kitchen.

'How is she?'

'Tina? Finding her mother hard to deal with,' Clare
told him.

'I'm not surprised. She can't cope at all. I think Tim
will want to get her transferred to the spinal injuries

unit at Stoke Mandeville—they have all the necessary social and emotional back-up as well as state-of-the-art technology for dealing with this sort of thing.' He sighed heavily and ran his hand through his hair. 'Are you doing anything tonight?'

She was caught off guard by the change of tack, because she had hardly seen anything of him since Monday night. He had been kept on the run by the events of the week, and there had been no opportunity to further their relationship—if indeed they had one, which after such a short time she doubted, but she admitted to herself that she hoped they could have. She met his eyes.

'Are you planning to jump my bones?' she said with a twinkle.

He gave a short, surprised laugh. 'Now that's a tempting idea!'

She blushed. 'I didn't really mean that the way it came out,' she laughed.

His hand came up and grazed her cheek. 'What a shame,' he teased gently. 'I've been invited to a party at the house of one of the consultants, and I hardly know anyone who'll be going—I'll be like a fish out of water.'

'Is it the Hamiltons?'

He nodded. 'Yes, that's right—they've just got married and they're throwing a party to celebrate. I gather they had a very quiet wedding and this is in lieu of a reception. Well, will you come with me?'

Clare smiled. 'I'm going anyway—Lizzi invited me. We're sort of friends—or as close to it as anyone is with her. She's always been a very private person until now. I can't believe the change Ross has made in her.'

'People don't change other people, they just give

them the confidence to be themselves—or take it
away.' He cupped her cheeks. 'So you'll come with
me?'

She nodded. 'I'd love to. I wasn't really looking
forward to it because I don't know all that many people
there myself. They're all a bit exalted, really.'

He laughed. 'I thought you said there was no
hierarchy?'

'Well, there isn't really, but most of the people
who'll be there are older than me or married——'

'Not part of the singles set, you mean?'

She shot him a surprised look. 'I'm not part of the
"singles set", Michael,' she said reprovingly.

'No, of course not, you don't have a lover and you
don't want one.'

She met his laughing eyes. 'Are you teasing me?'

He remained deadpan, except for the eyes. 'Would
I?'

'Yes, you would!'

'Perhaps a little.' His face gentled into a smile. 'What
time shall I pick you up?'

'I'm on a split, so I won't be ready to go until after
nine—does that matter?'

He shook his head. 'That's fine. I don't imagine it
will get off the ground much before then, anyway. Tell
you what, I'll go and get changed when I finish here,
and I'll come up to your flat and wait for you—how's
that?'

Too intimate, she wanted to say, but Sister O'Brien
came into the kitchen and smiled cheerily at them.

'Making coffee for that poor woman?'

Clare flushed guiltily, 'Yes, I was, Sister.'

Michael winked at her over Mary O'Brien's frilly

cap. 'We'll leave it like that, then, Staff,' he said and sauntered out, giving her no option but to agree.

She was just putting the finishing touches to her make-up when she heard the knock on her door at five past nine. 'Come in,' she called, and carried on with her face.

Glancing up in the mirror seconds later, she saw Michael lounging in her bedroom doorway, hands thrust deep into the pockets of his immaculate cream trousers. The cornflower-blue silk shirt he wore was the same shattering colour as his eyes, and in the V at the neck she could see a cluster of golden curls nestling in the hollow of his throat. He looked ruggedly male and devastatingly sexy. She blinked and smudged her mascara.

'Damn.' Picking up a tissue, she wiped the offending mascara off her lid and touched up the shadow.

'Sorry—didn't mean to startle you,' he apologised with a grin. Her heart flipped and she had to make a conscious effort to steady her hand.

Giving up, she dropped the eyeshadow brush and stood up, smoothing down the skirt of her cotton lawn dress. It was a splashy floral print in warm pastel shades, the perfect complement to her pale gold hair and English rose complexion, and she loved it.

'Will I do?' she asked with a twirl, and was rewarded by the bright flare of interest in his eyes.

'Oh, yes, you'll do,' he said with wry emphasis. 'My blood-pressure must have gone up to over two hundred in the last thirty seconds. Come on, out of here before I do something you'll make me regret!'

She scooped up her shawl and bag, and clicked her heels.

'Ready when you are, sir!'

'That's what I like—a woman who knows her place!'

He ushered her out to the car, and all the way to the Hamiltons' house she was conscious of him as she had never been before.

'What a fabulous place!' she breathed as Michael parked the car on the sloping lawn and led her across to the sprawling, split-level house.

'Gorgeous, isn't it? He must be stinking rich.'

'He's quite old—thirty-eight or -nine.'

'Oh, ancient!' Michael said with a laugh. 'I can assure you I won't have accumulated this sort of wealth in five years.'

'Private practice?'

He laughed and shook his head. 'Too busy with the boat. Maybe later.'

He ushered her through the front door, and they were greeted by their host and hostess, looking wonderfully relaxed and blissfully happy. They made a beautiful couple, Lizzi with her astonishing violet eyes and pale blonde hair, Ross tall and distinguished, his thick, prematurely silver hair a perfect foil for the healthy glow of his skin.

Clare hugged Lizzi warmly. 'Congratulations, Mrs Hamilton!' she said, her voice full of emotion.

Lizzi hugged her back. 'Thanks, Clare. I'm glad you could come. Ross, do you know Clare Stevens? She's Mary O'Brien's staff nurse.'

Ross shook her hand, and Clare was struck again by the wealth of warmth and understanding in his gentle grey-green eyes.

'Take care of her, she's a super girl,' Clare admonished him.

'Oh, I intend to cherish her until she begs for mercy,'

he said with a laugh, but she noticed his eyes met Lizzi's in a look so intensely private and filled with passionate commitment that she felt almost embarrassed to have witnessed it. He turned to Michael. 'Hello, Michael. Glad you could make it. Go on through and make yourselves at home. Drinks are in the kitchen—Callum will help you.'

'Who's Callum?' Michael asked as they walked away.

'Ross's oldest son. He's been married before.'

They collected their drinks and made their way out into the garden and down the terrace of steps.

'Lord, a pool!'

'Oh, yes—all mod cons! I expect things will deteriorate later and at least one person will end up chucked in—it was Lizzi last time!'

He chuckled. 'Remind me to keep well out of the way—these shoes wouldn't survive a dunking. Now,' he said, tucking his arm round her waist and guiding her away from the crowd, 'what's a lovely young thing like you doing all on your own at a party like this?'

'I'm not,' she reminded him.

'Ah, but you would have been if I hadn't turned up in the nick of time. So why? You can't tell me no one's offered?'

She shrugged. 'I didn't want to give anyone the wrong impression.'

'Meaning?'

'Meaning that if I go to a party with someone, that someone might get the wrong idea——'

'But you're here with me. Aren't you afraid I'll get the wrong idea?'

'No.' She turned to face him and met his gaze unblinkingly. 'You have the same problem—because you look the way you do, no one will take you seriously. I know you understand,' she told him frankly.

'That doesn't make me immune to your charms,' he said softly.

'Michael, don't. . .'

'OK, OK!' He held up his hands in laughing surrender. 'I take the hint. Now, who are all these people?'

They circulated, Clare introducing Michael to those people that she knew, and in turn being introduced herself to others who she knew only by sight. By ten-thirty they had talked themselves hoarse, and there was a welcome interruption when the music was turned down and Oliver Henderson, one of the other consultants, called everyone's attention from the top of the steps.

'Ladies and gentlemen,' he began, 'I don't want to bore you with speeches, but I'm sure you would all like me to take this opportunity to thank the Hamiltons for their hospitality tonight, and to wish them every happiness in their marriage. Ladies and gentlemen, I give you Ross and Lizzi!'

'Ross and Lizzi!' everyone chorused, and then there were yells of 'Speech!' from the crowd.

Ross came forward, his arm anchored round Lizzi's waist, and waved them all down.

'I don't want to make any speeches—I hate doing it nearly as much as Oliver does, but we would like to thank you for your good wishes, and the welcome I've received since joining the hospital. So much has happened since then that I can hardly believe it's only been ten weeks, but as all of it's been good I won't ask any questions!' There was a ripple of laughter, and he continued, 'Anyway, thank you all, and do enjoy yourselves.'

There was a round of enthusiastic applause, and then four young men appeared at Ross's side.

One of them was Mitch Baker, his registrar, and one was Ross's son Callum. He grinned at Ross and held up his hand.

'Ladies and gentlemen, for my favourite stepmother, the moment you've all been waiting for!'

Then they picked Ross up, ran down the steps and hurled him, yelling wildly, into the swimming pool.

'Good grief!' Michael muttered.

Clare was convulsed with laughter.

'Serves him right,' she said eventually. 'At the last party they had, he chucked Lizzi in in her underwear!'

'Why?'

She shrugged. 'No one knows, but we all have a fair idea!'

The music was turned up again, and as Ross climbed out of the pool and laughingly tossed his sons in over his shoulder, Michael pulled Clare into his arms.

'Dance with me,' he murmured.

'But it's a fast record!' she laughed.

'So halve the beat! Where's your imagination, Staff Nurse Stevens?'

There was a shriek behind them as Ross reached Lizzi and carried her, kicking and screaming, into the water, but Michael and Clare were oblivious.

The music changed tempo, and in the dimly lit garden Clare's arms reached up and twined round Michael's neck. His cheek rested against her hair, and as their bodies swayed gently to the music she relaxed against him and let herself go.

What harm could it do? She'd told him clearly enough that she wasn't in the market for an affair, and she carefully blanked off the part of her mind that told her things might be changing.

His hands rested lightly against her spine, and for a long time they danced without any conscious thought. Then Michael lifted his head and rested his brow against hers, and eased her closer with a subtle pressure of his hands.

'I think I'm going to die if I don't kiss you soon,' he murmured.

So much for her relaxation! So much for her belief that it couldn't do any harm! And the worst thing was, she didn't care any more.

'Me, too,' she whispered.

He drew in a sharp breath, and swallowed hard.

'Let's get out of here.'

Her heart pounding, she nodded blindly.

'Any sign of our host and hostess?' he asked, and she noticed his voice was strained.

'I don't think so.' Heavens, she didn't sound much better!

'Let's just go—they won't miss us. We'll thank them next week.'

Her wrap was still in the car, so they were able to make their way around the side of the house and leave without drawing attention to themselves.

All the way back to his cottage her heart was pounding with nerves, and as they pulled up outside, she took a deep, steadying breath before climbing out of the car.

Michael unlocked the front door and ushered her inside, then, leaning on the door, he pulled her gently but firmly back into his arms and kissed her thoroughly.

'I'm scared,' she whispered.

'Don't be. I won't do anything to hurt you, or

anything you don't want me to do. I just had to be alone with you, without an audience of interested spectators making notes on our every move.'

He let her go, and she stood trembling by the door as he went into the kitchen and put the kettle on.

'Coffee?' he asked, sticking his head back round the door, and then came towards her, a serious but tender expression on his face.

'Clare, it's OK. Do you want to go home?'

She shook her head numbly.

'Just hold me,' she said unsteadily, and he wrapped his arms around her and held her hard against his chest.

After a minute she relaxed, and he eased away from her, dropping a light kiss on her brow. 'Go and sit down, and I'll bring the coffee through. How do you take yours?'

'White, no sugar,' she told him, and moved mechanically into the sitting-room.

He joined her a few minutes later, sat down on the settee and patted the cushion beside him.

'Come and sit with me.'

His tone was gentle, persuasive, and quite unthreatening. Clare did as she was told, perching on the edge, longing to lean back against his side and at the same time ready to run if necessary.

His hand reached out and brushed the bare skin at the nape of her neck.

'Please don't be afraid of me,' he murmured.

'I—I'm not. I think I'm afraid of myself.'

'Don't be. I'll take care of you. Come here.'

He took her shoulders in his hands and eased her slowly back against him, so that she half sat, half lay across his lap. Then with one arm under her shoulders, he cradled her against his chest and sighed with contentment.

After a moment, in which she realised he was not about to make any demands of her, she slipped off her shoes and lifted her feet up on to the settee, snuggling closer to him.

'OK?'

'Mmm.' She moved her eyes and rested her cheek against his chest. His heart was beating steadily, slowly and evenly.

'You must be very fit,' she murmured.

He chuckled. 'Why?'

'Your heart beats very slowly—about fifty-five a minute—like an athlete's.'

'I jog some mornings, and windsurf, and I also play squash three times a week and tennis in the summer. When I'm not doing any of those things, I'm sailing. I suppose that keeps me fit. What about you?'

'Me? I'm lazy,' she said with a sigh of contentment.

'Like the cat.'

'Where is your cat?'

'Around. He's having a fantastic time exploring. He'll be in in a while for a bit of TLC, then off out again hunting. He's a bit of an alley cat, really, but he's an old softie underneath. His name's O'Malley, from the cat in *The Aristocats*.'

Right on cue, she heard a loud miaow and something heavy landed on her stomach. Her lids flew up and she peered, startled, straight into pair of bright blue eyes.

'He's a Siamese!'

'Oh, yes. Didn't I tell you that?'

O'Malley squawked and stepped delicately over her shoulder, taking up residence around Michael's neck.

'He thinks he's a collar,' Michael said in resignation.

Clare laughed and swivelled round so that her feet were back on the floor. 'He's very beautiful.'

'He's a rogue,' Michael said affectionately, and scratched his ears. The cat squawked again, and began to purr loudly.

They drank their coffee in companionable silence, broken only by the sound of O'Malley's tongue rasping over his paws. After a while he detached himself from Michael's neck and stalked out of the door, tail held high.

'He's off on the razzle again. More coffee?'

She shook her head. Somehow, without O'Malley's unwitting guardianship, she felt much more alone with Michael again.

'Do you want me to take you home?' he asked with gentle insight.

She looked up, startled. 'But I thought. . .'

'What?'

She shook her head. 'Nothing.'

His fingers traced the outline of her jaw, and threaded under her hair to knead the tense muscles of her neck.

'I want to make love to you, Clare, but there's more than that with us, isn't there?'

She met his eyes, surprised by his admission. 'Is there? For you, I mean?'

'Oh, yes. . .' His fingers closed around her shoulder and eased her gently back against him. 'Oh, yes, my love, there's much more. I think we could have something really special, and I think it deserves to be given time to flourish.' His lips brushed hers briefly, and with a sigh he hugged her and then let her go.

'Come on, I'd better take you home before you

undermine my good intentions and I do something
unspeakably wicked to you on the carpet.'

Clare giggled. 'You wouldn't!'

'Is that a dare?'

She shook her head, suddenly breathless, because
for all the lightness of his tone his eyes were deadly
serious. 'No. Take me home, Michael.'

With a wry grin, he helped her to her feet and led
her to the car.

Once they had set off he found her hand in the
darkness and rested it on his thigh, holding it there
except when he needed to change gear. When they
reached the hospital, he pulled up in the car park
outside the nurses' residence and turned to face her.

'How about spending the day with me tomorrow on
the boat?'

'I might be working,' she teased.

'But you're not—I checked the rota. If you don't
want to, you can always say no, Clare.'

She was struck by the uncertainty in his voice, and
squeezed his hand. 'Of course I want to. It would be
lovely.'

'Can you be ready by eight?'

'Yes, that's fine. What shall I wear?'

'Something scruffy and fairly warm, and bring shorts
and a swimsuit.' He leant over and kissed her firmly
but briefly, then pushed open the door. 'I won't come
in with you—I'm not sure I could resist the temptation.
I'll see you tomorrow. Sleep well, my love.'

'You too. Thanks for a lovely evening.'

She touched his cheek with her hand, and then
climbed out of the car and shut the door, watching
until his tail-lights disappeared from view.

Then she let herself back inside and prepared for

bed, certain she wouldn't be able to sleep. So he thought they could have something really special, something that deserved time to flourish. She wondered where it would lead—to heartache, or to a lifetime of happiness? Maybe neither. Only time would tell.

She snuggled down in bed, her head crowded with images of Michael, and fell asleep in seconds.

'Oh, Michael, she's lovely!'

Clare stood on the quayside and gazed in admiration at the little sloop. Built on traditional, classic lines, she was sleek and graceful, and Clare fell in love on the spot.

Michael slammed the boot of the Volvo and strolled to her side, a confident, cocky grin on his face. 'Isn't she great? I know every inch of her, inside and out—I helped my grandfather build her the year I was ten. She handles beautifully—he really knew what he was doing. Come on, let's get all this stuff stowed and take her out.'

He led Clare on to the pontoon that ran out like a finger into the marina, with little branches off it at intervals to which boats were moored in orderly profusion.

'I may be biased, but I think she's the prettiest,' Clare told him as they arrived at the *Henrietta* and she got her first close look at the boat.

'I'm biased too, but I happen to agree with you!' He shot her a cheeky grin. 'Here, hold this lot.' He handed her some bags and hopped nimbly aboard, uncovering the cockpit and stowing the cover neatly under the seat in the stern.

Then he took the bags from her, dropped them into

the cockpit and held out his hands. 'Welcome aboard,' he said, and as she leapt forward he caught her under her arms and swung her on to the deck.

She fell against him, laughing, and as she straightened his head came down and he kissed her lingeringly.

'Good morning,' he said huskily.

'Good morning yourself,' she replied, suddenly breathless. 'What can I do?'

He waved a hand at the bags. 'Get all this lot stowed away in the cabin and come back and keep me company.'

She scrambled somewhat inelegantly over the high step of the hatchway, down the two rungs of the companionway into the main cabin, and took a deep breath.

Oh, yes. Varnish, and seawater, and diesel, and the unmistakable smell of the bilges. Clare hadn't realised how much she had missed messing about in boats until she had caught that evocative smell. Heavens, it took her right back to her childhood! Suddenly light-hearted, she looked around her.

On her right was a desk next to a bank of navigational equipment, charts, radio and so on, and on her left a little galley, with a gimballed stove designed to remain stable as the boat tilted from side to side. In front of her was the main seating area, with two long benches down either side that would convert to berths, one L-shaped, with a fixed table in front of it that would collapse to make a double berth.

There was a door directly opposite her that led, she imagined, to another little cabin in the bows, and the 'head', that ghastly contraption that passed for a loo on board small boats.

She looked around her at the cabin, and a little smile touched her mouth. This was Michael.

There were a few books—Nicholas Monsarrat, Neville Shute, Hammond Innes—a couple of bottles of wine and one of brandy, two jars of coffee and some powdered milk, a few tins of staples—everything a man like him would need for a quick getaway.

She heard his light tread behind her and turned.

'Are you a loner?'

He looked startled for a second, and then smiled. 'No, not really, but I do need to escape every now and again and top up. Will that worry you?'

There he goes again, talking as if we have a future, she thought with a soaring heart.

'No, it won't worry me at all. We all need solitude periodically.'

He gave her a brief hug. 'What do you think of her?'

'Oh, she's lovely—just right. All wooden fittings and personal touches—not at all like a modern boat.'

He laughed. 'You don't sound as if you approve of modern boats!'

'Well, they have their place, I suppose, but they're characterless by comparison.'

'Thank you,' he said simply, and hugged her again. After a moment he eased away from her with a reluctant sigh and headed for the hatch. 'We need to get under way if we're going to catch the tide up the Deben. There's a sand-spit across the mouth of the river that closes it off at low tide, but if we go now we should make it just about right.'

She found a picnic in one of the bags and wedged it in the corner of the galley, and dropped the other bag, full of towels and sweaters, on the quarter bunk under the cockpit. Then she clambered back over the hatch to join Michael.

'There's a light breeze picking up—just do us nicely,' he said, and pressed the starter button. The engine turned, coughed, and fired immediately. He cast off, jumped nimbly back on board and steered her carefully over to the lock. The top gates were open, and the lads working the lock made her fast and stood by to steady the boat as she lowered.

'Tide's only just coming in now, so we've got quite a long way to go. Will it worry you?'

Clare shook her head. 'Must make it tricky if you get back too late,' she said. 'Do you have to find another mooring outside overnight?'

'Oh, no—they have a motto here, "Lock around the Clock"—you can come and go whenever you please. Just as well—when I got her here from the Scillies it was nearly midnight.'

'Isn't that a bit hair-raising in the dark, in strange waters?'

He laughed. 'Hardly strange! She's been moored near here for fifteen years—my grandfather lives in Holbrook. I know this coast like the back of my hand.'

As the lock gates opened and Michael manoeuvred the boat out into the estuary, Clare sat back and relaxed. There was nothing she could usefully do, and Michael was clearly competent. She might as well give herself a treat and watch him at work.

And it was a treat, she admitted to herself some time later. He had changed into ragged cut-off jeans and abandoned his T-shirt, and she watched the smooth play of muscle in his back as he hoisted the mainsail and unfurled the foresail, tightening the sheets and bringing the head round into the wind.

'OK?'

She nodded. 'Super. I'd forgotten how much I love it!'

He laughed in sheer enjoyment. 'Great, isn't it? I'd die if I couldn't do this!'

After a while he offered her the helm, and stood behind her, his hands steady on hers, his chest brushing lightly against her back. She leant back against him, resting her head on his shoulder, and made a small sound of contentment in her throat.

'Happy?'

'Oh, Michael, you have no idea. . .'

His lips nuzzled her neck. 'You taste wonderful—fresh and clean and delicious. Mind the ferry.'

'What ferry?'

He laughed. 'Just testing. Want to take her round the point?'

She let out a breath. 'I'll try—just don't go away.'

'I won't. Take your time.'

She took a steadying breath, let out the port sheet, spun the wheel and hauled in the starboard sheet. *Henrietta* yawed wildly for a second or two, then the sails filled with a slap and she settled down on the new course.

'Well done.'

She laughed breathlessly. 'It was awful!'

He chuckled, his arms wrapping round her waist to pull her back against him. 'It wasn't perfect, but it was fine. You'll do, with practice.'

'Hmm. Maybe another time. Over to you, Cap'n Bligh.'

She slid under his arm and sat in the cockpit, her feet propped on the other seat, and mopped up the sunshine. After a few minutes she started to overheat,

and went below to put on her shorts and T-shirt. There
was a cooling breeze off the sea, but it was going to be
a gloriously hot June day nevertheless.

Michael's eyes ran appreciatively over her legs as she
climbed over the hatch, and he gave a gusty sigh.

'How the hell am I supposed to keep my hands off
you when you look like that?'

'Well, ditto!'

Their eyes met.

'Oh, dear God, Clare—I want you,' he whispered.

She swallowed. 'Can we talk about this later? You're
going to run us aground on the sand-spit if you don't
concentrate!'

He swore softly under his breath, and then gave a
rueful chuckle. 'It's a deal. Just sit down and don't
fidget about, or I won't stand a chance of thinking
straight!'

It was a wonderful day. They tacked up the river
towards Woodbridge, ate their picnic in sight of the
Tide Mill, and dropped back down with the tide,
rounding the point off Felixstowe at four o'clock. By
five they were back in the marina, mooring *Henrietta*
and packing up their things.

By the time they left, Clare's nerves were at screaming pitch. Every touch of his hand, every brush of his
body against hers as they manoeuvred round each
other in the little cabin had left her senses reeling.

They drove back to the cottage in a potent silence,
and when they arrived back, he stilled her hand as he
moved to unload the car.

'Leave that lot. I want to make love to you. I've
been watching you bending around in those tiny little
shorts for hours, and I really don't think I can stand
much more of it.'

Her heart was pounding as she followed him into the cottage and up the stairs. In his bedroom he turned to her, his hands cupping her shoulders lightly. His eyes searched her face, his expression serious. 'Is this what you want, Clare?'

She nodded, beyond speech.

'Are you sure?'

She nodded again. 'I'm terrified—I've never done it before, and I don't really know what to expect, and I'll probably be a dreadful disappointment to you, but yes—I'm sure.'

'Oh, my love. . .'

He was so gentle, so careful with her, his hands tender, his voice coaxing her softly. And it was easy— much easier than she had imagined, and so—beautiful wasn't the word, it was too earthy, too positive for that, but as she reached the crest, something deep inside her shattered and she felt freer than she had ever felt before.

Dear God, I love him! she thought, and clung to him as his body quivered under her hands and he cried her name.

CHAPTER THREE

'I THOUGHT we were going to give this relationship time to flourish,' Clare said sleepily, much later.

Beneath her ear Michael's chest rumbled gently with suppressed laughter. 'Yes, well, it flourished quicker than I dared to hope.'

He levered himself up on one elbow and looked down at her, his face gravely tender. 'Are you all right?'

'I'm fine. I've never felt so good in my life.'

'I'm glad. Neither have I.'

'Oh, come on,' she laughed self-consciously. 'I didn't know what I was doing——'

'Yes, you did. You were making love. It doesn't require technical competence, darling.' He kissed her gently, his voice roughened with emotion. 'You were wonderful—warm, generous, funny—I love you, Clare.'

Her eyes filled with tears. 'Oh, Michael, I love you too.'

She clung to him, her heart overflowing with happiness. She didn't understand how it could have happened so soon, but it had, and it seemed so right loving him, as if she had been waiting all this time for him to come along and fill her life with sunshine and laughter.

He kissed her lingeringly, his hands tracing lazy patterns on her skin, and she tentatively laid her palms against his chest.

'That feels good,' he murmured.

46

'Can I touch you?' she asked hesitantly.

He flopped on to his back and spread his arms wide with a wicked grin. 'Do whatever you want—I'm yours!'

His laugh turned to a groan as she ran her fingertips experimentally down the centre of his chest. His eyes closed, he lay rigid while she explored the changing textures and planes of hair and skin, tracing the smooth line of muscle and sinew, revelling in the feel of satin over steel. Fascinated by the contrast between vulnerability and strength, she dallied over the jut of his hipbones and the slight hollow of his pelvis above the taut, hard muscles of his thighs. His legs were strong and straight, well-muscled and smoothly tanned beneath the dense scatter of blond curls.

She knelt by his feet, her fingers tracing each toe in turn, smoothing the strong arch as her eyes trailed slowly up his body, absorbing his beauty like a drug.

'You're perfect,' she said huskily, 'so perfect. A perfect hero!'

He laughed self-consciously and reached down to pull her over him.

'I've got scarry knees,' he confessed.

'So? All little boys have scarry knees. They probably aren't any worse than mine.'

'Shut up and kiss me,' he commanded softly, and she bent her head and laid her lips against his.

'I love you,' she murmured, and with a ragged groan he rolled her beneath him and took her with him to heaven.

They climbed off the high old-fashioned bedstead at midnight, raided the fridge and took the feast up to bed with them, pausing in the middle to make love again. They fell asleep as the early fingers of dawn crawled over the horizon, and woke again at eight, ready to take on the world.

'Do you know how to windsurf?' he asked her.

Clare, feeling like the cat that got the canary, shook her head contentedly without bothering to open her eyes. 'Sounds energetic.'

'It is—would you like me to teach you?'

She forced an eye open. 'Now?'

'Maybe in a little while,' he laughed.

It was another hour before the world penetrated their little cocoon, and then Michael chivvied her through the bathroom and into her clothes.

'You're hassling me,' she complained gently.

'You need hassling to stop you getting side-tracked— it's only self-defence, I'm exhausted!'

She giggled wickedly.

'Oh, no—come on, out!'

He shooed her into the Volvo, loaded up the roof-rack with the board, and they set off for the reservoir.

'It's harder than it looks!' she said ruefully later on, after yet another ignominious dunking.

'It's a bit windy for learning. Do you want to try again?'

She shook her head. 'I'll just sit here and watch you—it's better for my ego!'

He was good—very good, she acknowledged, study-ing him and the other windsurfers as they tacked back and forth across the water. She smiled with great self-satisfaction.

She was still smiling when he rejoined her.

'OK?'

'Very impressive. Can I join your fan-club?'

He dropped on the grass beside her and blotted his

wet hair with a towel. 'It's very exclusive—only one member so far.'

'Will she mind if I join?' Clare asked, shocked at the little twist of jealousy.

'He—O'Malley. No one else has been invited. No, I don't suppose he'll mind, although he might get a bit miffed if I keep throwing him off the bed all night.'

She laughed. 'I refuse point blank to share you with a cat,' she told him.

'Possessive, eh?'

She faltered, her confidence a little rocked for a moment. 'Do you mind?'

He lifted his hand and rubbed his knuckles over her cheek. 'No, love, I don't mind. I feel the same way about you. I want you all to myself forever.'

She met his eyes, startled. 'Forever?'

He nodded, slowly. 'I think so. It certainly feels like that to me.'

She reached up her hand and wrapped it round his wrist, turning her face into his palm and kissing it. 'To me, too. The thought of my life without you in it now is unbearable. I feel as if I've know you for years, not less than a week.'

'You have known me for years—I'm your other half. We just haven't met until now.' He lifted her face and she thought she would drown in the love she saw there in his eyes. 'Marry me, Clare. Stay with me forever.'

'Oh, yes. . .oh, Michael, yes!'

She flung her arms around his neck and hugged him, revelling in the hard strength of his body and the steady thud of his heart against her ribs.

Then he let her go, pulling her to her feet and gathering up all their things. 'Come on, we'll go and see my grandfather and tell him the news. He's been nagging me for years to settle down.'

The old man was obviously delighted at his grandson's unexpected visit, and welcomed him with open arms. The sight of Michael hugging him with such affection brought a lump to her throat.

Michael eased away from the old man and beckoned to Clare.

'Pop, I've brought someone special to meet you. Her name's Clare. Clare, this is Pop.'

The old man turned sightless eyes towards her, and Clare realised with a sudden shock that he was blind. He held out his hands, and she took them firmly, standing still while he stared blindly at her, finally nodding.

'What colour's your hair?'

'Blonde.'

'Your eyes?'

'Grey——'

'They're the colour of the early morning mist on still water,' Michael corrected.

'My grandson always was an old romantic. May I touch your face?'

She smiled. 'Of course.'

His gnarled old hands explored her features gently, and then he grunted with satisfaction. 'Good strong chin. You'll need that to deal with this young scamp. Do you love him?'

'Yes, I do, very much.'

He turned away abruptly. 'Been out on *Henrietta* recently, boy?'

'Yes, we went out yesterday.'

'You took Clare?'

Michael winked at her. 'Yes, I did. She's got the makings of a good sailor.'

'Humph. Must be love—none of his other women has been allowed near her.'

He shuffled across to his chair and sat down with a sigh. 'Let's have a cup of tea, then, Michael—go and put the kettle on.'

'Aye, aye, Cap'n!' Michael snapped to attention, winked at Clare again and left the room.

'So, how did you meet my grandson?'

'He's working at the same hospital as me. We met on Monday.' Less than a week, she realised in surprise.

'Not long, then. Still, if it's right you know straight away, I reckon. Knew the moment I clapped eyes on Lottie that she was the girl for me. Don't suppose Michael's any different. Has he asked you to marry him yet?'

'As a matter of fact, I have,' Michael told him, coming back into the room, 'and she very sensibly said yes.'

His grandfather snorted. 'That remains to be seen. So, my girl, do you intend to make him a good wife? Can you cook? Keep the house clean, do his washing, that sort of thing? A man needs to be looked after, you know, and you'll have to make sure you keep your looks—it's no damn good if he doesn't want to come home to his own bed, you know! Don't want the lad straying because you let yourself go.'

She blushed. 'Of course I can cook and clean— probably just as well as Michael,' she said spiritedly, 'and I have no plans to let myself go. As for Michael, if he "strays", it will be because there's something wrong in our marriage, and it will be up to both of us to put it right.'

The old man cackled and slapped his leg. 'Well said, young lady, well said. You'll do. Michael, show her the kitchen. I want to talk to you while she makes the tea.'

She fled gratefully.

'Sorry about that,' Michael said ruefully. 'I tried to catch your eye to warn you he was winding you up, but you were so busy glaring at him you didn't see me.'

She laughed weakly. 'I thought he was serious. Michael, what sort of a marriage *do* you have in mind?' she asked him, suddenly unsure of him. She seemed to know so little about him.

'A partnership,' he said gently, pulling her into his arms. 'Sharing the duties and responsibilities of the home, talking through our problems, standing by each other. Does that answer your question?'

'How important is faithfulness to you?'

He went quite still. 'It's fundamental, Clare. I'll never be unfaithful to you, as long as we're together.'

She hugged him. 'Thank you. That's just what I needed to hear. Right, go and talk to him and tell him not to wind me up, and I'll play mother and make the tea.' She gave him a little push towards the door, and turned towards the kettle, humming softly to herself.

The rest of the afternoon was uneventful. They had tea in the garden, and she admired the roses and the honeysuckle, and Pop told her about Lottie, Michael's grandmother, and the children they had raised in the house.

'It's too big for me now, but I don't want to move. I'll stay here now till the end, then they can do what they like with it when I'm gone. I shan't care then.'

He fell silent, staring at some inner vision, and then he straightened. 'Time for my nap. You two young

A PERFECT HERO 53

things run along and enjoy yourselves—and remember what I said, Michael.'

'I will, Pop. How would you like to go for a sail next weekend?'

'See how I go. Give me a ring, boy—anyone would think the damn phone had been cut off the way you don't keep in touch!'

He apologised, helped the old man into the house and then they left.

'Is he really all right on his own?' Clare asked worriedly.

Michael sighed. 'No, but he won't move. He's a stubborn old fool, but I love him.'

'I can see that. Are you close to your father?'

'Not really. Not like that. It was always Pop I turned to for advice, and of course, being retired, he had time for me when my father didn't. I used to spend all my holidays here with them, and when Grannie died, I felt he needed me even more. It was difficult during my training and espcially in my house year, but despite what he says, I'm never out of touch for more than a couple of days. Sometimes I think he forgets I've rung him.'

They went back to the cottage, cooked a simple meal and talked until after midnight. Then Clare yawned. 'Sorry,' she said with a rueful smile. 'Not enough sleep last night.'

'I'd better take you home. Not that I want to, I'll miss having you beside me, but I suppose we ought to act a little conventionally, especially as you live in the hospital. Before you go, I want to give you this.'

He fished in his pocket and came up with a little square leather box. He lifted the lid, and inside, nestled on faded blue velvet, was an old ring, a row of aquamarines and seed pearls in a very simple setting. Clare reached out a finger and touched it hesitantly.

'Oh, Michael, it's. . .' She trailed off, lost for words.

'If you don't like it,' he said quickly, 'I'll happily buy you one—anything you like, diamonds—whatever——'

'No! Oh, no, it's lovely—is it very old? Where did you get it?'

'It was Grannie's. Pop thought I should give it to you. He said you'd appreciate it.'

'Lottie's?' Clare felt tears start to her eyes. 'Michael—are you sure?'

'Of course I'm sure. Why, aren't you?'

'Oh, I'm absolutely certain. I have no doubts at all. I'm just having trouble believing it. I have to keep pinching myself.'

'Idiot! Believe it—it's true.'

He lifted her left hand and slipped the ring on to her finger. 'Perfect. He said it would fit. You won't be able to wear it for work, of course, but you can always put it on a chain around your neck.'

'Or through my nose,' she teased.

He met her eyes, his own serious. 'It's not a shackle, Clare. It's an invitation to share my life, with all its ups and downs. It may be a bumpy ride, but I can promise you it'll never be boring.'

'I accept,' she said, with a hiccuping little laugh, and flung her arms round him.

It was much later before he eventually took her back to the hospital, and as she slipped into bed she had to touch the ring to remind herself that it wasn't all a wonderful, fleeting dream.

* * *

She was almost late on duty in the morning. Mary O'Brien arrived as she did, and Clare was certain the keen-eyed woman would miss nothing of the meteoric changes that must be echoed in her eyes. As it was she gave her a cursory glance, a friendly smile and said, 'Good weekend? You've caught the sun.'

Clare blushed. 'Lovely, thank you. How was yours?'

'Oh, busy. Had my daughter for the weekend with the baby. Honestly, Clare, I'd forgotten how much running around you have to do. Goodness knows how I coped with four!'

They laughed, and went into the office, where the night sister was getting ready to give the report.

'Morning, all,' Sister O'Brien said cheerfully. 'OK, Sister Price, what's been going on?'

One of the elderly ladies with a hip replacement had had a pulmonary embolus and was on Heparin, another was showing signs of pressure sores because she had been bed-ridden for so long. She was to be got up and kept up as much as she could tolerate it, and the physiotherapist was working on getting her mobile as quickly as possible.

Tina White had gone, transferred to Stoke Mandeville over the weekend by helicopter, and Pete Sawyer was progressing well, although it was too soon to tell if the bone graft would do its job.

Danny, as usual, had been a total pain in the neck.

'The sooner we get him up and out the better for everyone, I think!' Sister Price said with a laugh. 'Apart from that, there are two new admissions—Mrs Wright, a fifty-seven-year-old lady with a fracture of the left femoral neck following a fall, which Mr Mayhew pinned yesterday, and Mr Jones. He's forty-two, and was brought in with cracked ribs and a clean fracture

of the radius which has been immobilised in a cast.
He'll probably go home today. Right, I think that's
it—I'm off to bed. Have a lovely day!'

Sister O'Brien detailed Clare to do a training round
with the two first-year nurses on the care of patients in
traction. She was in the first bay with the elderly
patients discussing the importance of meticulous treatment of pressure areas when Michael appeared.

'Everything all right, Staff?' he asked with a wicked
grin.

'Fine, thank you, Mr Barrington.' She made herself
smile normally.

'Good. I'll catch up with you later—there's a new
procedure I've been wanting to try out—perhaps we
could discuss it over lunch?'

She struggled against the blush and failed. 'I would
think that would be fine.'

'Excellent. One o'clock in the coffee lounge?' He
gave her flushed skin a sympathetic glance. 'Warm in
here, isn't it?'

He sauntered off, whistling, to say hello to the lady
who had been his first patient. The nurses watched him
adoringly. Clare was disgusted and insanely jealous.
Damn it, they were almost drooling!

'If I could have your attention, ladies?' she said with
rather more sarcasm than she had intended, and they
apologised and gave her their undivided attention—
which actually made things rather difficult, as Clare's
thoughts had gone off at a decided tangent.

'Sue, perhaps you could recap for us?' she said in a
moment of inspiration.

The morning dragged. Clare switched her lunch
break with Sister O'Brien, and was in the coffee lounge
waiting when Michael came in with Tim Mayhew at

five past one, deep in conversation. He saw Clare, excused himself and came over to her.

'Hi,' he said softly. 'Sorry I'm late. Have you eaten?'

She shook her head.

'Come on, then, let's go and get something.'

When they were seated, she asked, 'So what was this new procedure, then?'

He gave a short, husky laugh. 'I though we'd discuss that later over supper at my place——'

She flushed as his meaning dawned on her. 'I changed my lunch break to come down here and meet you!'

He reached out and took her hand, ignoring all the interested glances they were getting. 'Didn't you want to have lunch with me?'

She snatched her hand away. 'Of course I did—what are you doing, holding my hand here? It'll be all round the hospital by half-past one!'

'So? Are you ashamed to be seen with me?'

She sighed, and smiled at him. 'No, of course I'm not ashamed to be seen with you.'

'Good. Look, I'm operating until after six tonight—have you got a car?'

'Uh-huh. Just a little Fiesta, but it does OK. Why?'

'Can you remember the way to the cottage?'

'Of course!'

He fished in his pocket and came up with a set of keys. Taking one off the ring, he slid it across the table towards her. 'Here, let yourself in and start supper—I'll be home about seven. Is that OK?'

She nodded and slipped the key into her pocket. 'Anything in particular you fancy?'

His smile widened, and she blushed a fiery red.

'I thought we were going to talk about that later?' he

said, a thread of laughter in his voice, and she shook her head in despair.

'You won't behave, will you?'

He chuckled. 'Life's too short. I must go, I've got a clinic and I need to go through the notes. See you later.'

He stood up, leant forward and dropped a kiss on her startled lips.

'Well, well! What have we here?'

'Oh! Hello, Lizzi. How are you? Got over the dunking?'

'Oh, that! Yes, I'm getting used to it! Mind if I join you? Ross is still in Theatre.'

She settled herself beside Clare, turned towards her and studied her thoughtfully. 'You look different,' she said finally, and Clare felt her skin heat again.

'Sorry,' Lizzi said contritely. 'It's just that in all the years I've known you, you've never had that smug, mellow look you have now.'

'Snap.'

Lizzi laughed. 'Oh, well, mine's due to love, among other things.' She prodded the food around on her plate. 'So, are you and Michael seeing each other?'

Clare was suddenly struck by the need to tell someone of the momentous events of the weekend. Only then, she felt, would it all become real.

'I spent the weekend with him,' she stated bluntly.

'Good God,' Lizzi said quietly. 'Was that wise? You hardly know him!'

'Probably not. It was all pretty sudden. He asked me to marry him.'

Lizzi's fork stopped in mid-air. 'He did *what*?'

'Asked me to marry him. I said yes. See.' She fished

in the neck of her uniform and pulled out the ring, suspended on the gold chain that had held her locket.

'Oh, Clare, it's beautiful! Oh, love, I am so pleased for you!'

'Don't tell anyone yet—I'm not sure how public he wants it just yet.'

'Can I tell Ross?'

'Tell Ross what?'

Ross, still dressed in Theatre greens, pushed Michael's plate out of the way and sat opposite them.

'Hello, darling. Nothing. You'll have to wait.'

'How boring. Have you missed me?'

'In four hours? Dreadfully!' Lizzi laughed.

Once again, Clare felt as if she was intruding, and excused herself to hurry back to the ward.

As soon as she was off duty she ran up to her flat, showered and changed, and put a clean dress into a carrier bag for the morning—just in case. She arrived at the cottage just after five, fed the cat, threw together a casserole and took a cup of tea in the garden to wait for Michael.

He was back just before seven and found her pulling up weeds in the shrubbery.

She sat back on her heels and smiled at him. 'Hi! You're early!'

'Easier than we thought. Makes a change. How's my favourite girl tonight?'

She stood up, brushed her grubby hands on her jeans and kissed him. 'Wonderful. Are you hungry? There's a casserole in the oven.'

'Fabulous. Let me shower and change and I'll be right down. Would you like to open a bottle of wine?'

Over the meal he asked her if she had told her parents about him yet.

'No, I haven't. I wasn't sure how public you wanted to make it yet.'

'Public as you like, darling. We'll put an announcement in the paper if you want.'

'Are you sure?'

He laid down his knife and fork. 'You keep asking me that. Are you sure yourself? If you aren't, then do say so.'

'Oh, no, I'm sure—I just can't believe my luck!'

He chuckled. 'I know the feeling. This is delicious— any more?'

And so they settled into the routine. The first one home prepared the meal, and they tackled the clearing up together. For the first few nights Clare got up and went back to the hospital to satisfy convention, but by the weekend they decided it was ridiculous.

On the Saturday morning Clare rang her parents and told them she was moving in with him. They were a bit surprised, but so pleased about their little girl finally taking the plunge that they said nothing.

They met him on Saturday evening after she came off duty, and fell under his spell as she was sure they would. On Sunday he took Pop sailing while she was working, and on Monday she tackled the housework while he went in to the hospital. He was home very late, having had to operate on a hang-glider pilot who had come a cropper, and slid into bed beside Clare with a contented sigh.

She was on an early on Tuesday, and took the report from Sister Price in the absence of Sister O'Brien, who was on days off until Thursday.

Danny Drew had been playing up in the night again, and had kept Pete Sawyer awake. He was still suffering with his arm, although his pelvis had healed well and his patella was well on the way to recovery. Mrs Wright, who had fallen the previous week, had also had a restless night and Clare made a note to get the SHO to have a look at her.

'There's one interesting new admission,' Sister Price told them. 'Barry Warner. He's a young man of twenty-four whose hang-glider folded up on him. He's got extensive fractures of just about everything, and needs very careful nursing. I suggest anyone coming into contact with him should look at the X-rays first. He had a compressed fracture of L4, and a right sacro-iliac strain, but otherwise no spinal injuries. Severe disloca-tion of the left shoulder, cracked acetabulum on the right due to the way he fell, but mostly it's lower leg fractures with external fixation on the right leg because of the soft tissue damage. Oh, and he cracked some bones in his right hand and wrist but they don't seem to be giving him much trouble. Apart from that he's a mass of cuts and bruises, and feeling thoroughly sorry for himself, but who can blame him with that lot?'

'I should say he's lucky to be alive,' Clare com-mented, and Sister Price laughed.

'Just now I don't think he'd agree with you, Staff. Mr Barrington's done a wonderful job of sticking him back together again. He was working on him until very late.'

'I know,' Clare said without thinking, and then rushed on, 'I spoke to him this morning, he told me about it.'

She blushed, and Sister Price raised an eyebrow. 'I didn't realise he was in yet. Any questions? No? Right, I'll be off. See you tomorrow.'

Clare could have kicked herself. The other nurses were exchanging speculative glances, and she sent them all off about their duties with rather more speed than was strictly necessary. Michael stuck his head round the door minutes later and blew her a kiss.

'Morning, gorgeous. Thanks for leaving me the coffee.'

'You're welcome. Sister Price thinks you're wonderful.'

'Of course! It's only to be expected. I am wonderful!'

'Modest, too,' she said with a smile. 'I gather you did amazing things to the young hang-glider.'

'Barry Warner? God, he was a mess. Have you seen him yet?'

'No, I was just going to go and have a look and make sure he was all right.' On their way to the little side-ward where Barry Warner was being nursed, she told him all about putting her foot in it, and he laughed.

'I don't know why you don't just tell them. Perhaps we should fix the date—how about a month? That give you long enough?'

She stopped in her tracks. 'Are you serious?'

'Of course I'm serious—I want to marry you. How many ways do I have to say it?'

'Shh, keep your voice down!' she hissed. 'I have to work here, and they're all bug-eyed with curiosity as it is.'

'So put them out of their misery,' he said with a grin. 'Tell them we're getting married on the first of August. That gives you six weeks or so.'

'Are we?' she said, surprised.

'Well, I don't know, but we could. Why not?'

'Why not, indeed!' she said with a laugh. 'Come on, Mr B, our patient awaits.'

He was a mess, Michael was right. His right leg was in traction to keep the pressure off the hip joint, and his left arm was strapped across his chest to immobilise his dislocated shoulder.

He was staring blankly out of the window, and turned listlessly towards them as they went into the room.

'Hello, Barry, how are you feeling?' Michael asked, picking up the charts from the foot of the bed and scanning them quickly.

'Everything hurts.'

'I'm afraid it will for a while. It's good news in a way because it means your nerves haven't suffered too much damage. I'll increase your pain relief. Let's have a look at your legs.'

He turned back the bedclothes and studied the mangled limbs in front of him in silence for a while. The left leg had a neat incision just beside the shin, and had been plated and pinned after open reduction. It was immobilised in a split cast to allow for swelling.

The right leg, which had extensive skin loss and so was unsuitable for internal fixation, had an external fixator in position, with threaded screws passing through into the bone fragments, holding them in line. It looked gruesome, but Clare knew that most patients tolerated the system very well. Because of the lower leg injuries, he was on skin traction to relieve the pressure on his hip joint, and his lower leg was resting in a 'gutter'.

'Looks good,' he told the young man. 'Can you wriggle your toes for me?'

He grimaced and managed to move them all slightly.

'Fingers? Excellent. Well done. The physiotherapist will be round to see you shortly so we can get things moving as soon as possible. You're lucky you didn't smash your heels, you know. That's the most common result of your type of landing.'

Barry turned his head away and didn't respond.

With a shrug Michael headed for the door. 'I'll come and see you again later, and we'll increase the pain relief now. I'll write it up in the office.'

They walked back to the nurses' station together, deep in conversation about the complicated management of Barry Warner's extensive injuries. As they reached the door of Sister's office, Tim Mayhew appeared and hailed them.

'Ah, this is the young lady!' he said in his penetrating voice. 'I gather you've captured my SR!'

Clare gave an embarrassed laugh. 'Something like that.'

'Or was it the other way round?'

He turned his deceptively soft brown eyes on Michael.

Michael grinned. 'A little of each, let's say. And captivated, rather than captured.'

'Well, whatever, I wish you both the very best. Now, tell me all about this young hang-glider. I gather from David Blake that you're a better surgeon than I am.'

'I wish!' Michael said with a laugh. 'He's too kind and not nearly observant enough if he thinks that, sir.'

Mr Mayhew shook his head. 'I don't think so. You're a damn fine surgeon, Michael. Given time and experience, you'll be world class. Of course you're not as conservative as me—I probably would have put the right leg in a gutter and left it at that, with a Steinmann's pin for the acetabulum, and tackled the tib and fib later on when the skin had healed. However, no harm in getting the healing process under way if possible. Shouldn't be surprised if we don't end up with a non-union. Got the X-rays?'

They went into the office, and Michael wrote up the increased rate of delivery of Pethidine through the automatic pump for Barry. Leaving them poring over the X-rays, Clare went back out to the nurses' station and asked the junior staff nurse, Deborah Lewis, to check the pump as she adjusted it.

'What was all that about?' Deborah asked curiously as they walked towards Barry's room.

Clare flushed. 'All what?' she said as vaguely as possible.

'Oh, come on! Rumour's rife, you know. You've moved out of your flat, every time he looks at you he nearly burns holes in you with those fabulous eyes—and then old Mayhew makes funny noises. Now give!'

Clare laughed and gave up. 'OK. Michael and I are getting married.'

'How exciting!' Deborah's eyes lit up. 'When?'

'I don't know—we haven't really decided. Probably the beginning of August.'

'That soon? You are a dark horse. We had no idea that you already knew him!'

'I didn't,' she said, and flushed again. 'We just—hit it off, right from the start.'

'You must have done,' Deborah said drily. 'Some people have all the luck. Oh, well. There's always David Blake.'

Clare chuckled. 'You could do worse. He's been after you for months.'

'Hmm.' Deborah wrinkled her nose. 'Was it Groucho Marx who said never belong to a club that will have you as a member? Let's check this pump.'

* * *

The rest of the week was uneventful but blissfully happy. She discovered a saxophone in his spare bedroom, and made him play it for her. He did, and she was enthralled. He did everything well, so she shouldn't have been surprised, but somehow she was.

His repertoire was wide and varied, ranging from sleazy jazz, through Mozart horn concertos, to soulful, haunting melodies that sent chills up her spine.

The days were made all the more exciting by the fact that they saw each other from time to time, and the nights—the nights defied description.

Clare had never been so happy in her life. On Thursday evening he took her windsurfing again, and she managed to stay up long enough to fall in love with the sensation of skimming over the water, the wind in her hair, muscles braced to balance the weight of the board. 'Fabulous!' she told him. 'I love it! We must do it again.'

'How about Saturday? Are you off this weekend?'

She nodded. 'Till Sunday lunchtime, anyway. Can we take *Henrietta* out?'

He laughed. 'You want it all, don't you?'

She threw back her hair and shook it, revelling in the feel of the sun on her face and the sound of his laughter.

'Yes, I want it all. Is that so wrong?'

'No.' He sobered, and reached out to take her in his arms. 'No, it's not wrong. I want it all, too. I just wonder if we're being greedy.'

Afterwards she wondered if they had known, if some sixth sense had warned them of what was coming, but she felt a chill run over her, and that night they made love with a desperate intensity that left them both shaken. They slept wrapped in each other's arms, as if together they could keep out whatever demon stalked them.

They were wrong.

CHAPTER FOUR

FRIDAY was hectic to start with. Several patients were going home, in time for the weekend, and they needed their notes writing up and drugs fetched from the pharmacy ready for their discharge.

Barry Warner had had a rotten night, and was desperately depressed. Clare did her best to cheer him up, but he was sullen and uncommunicative. The physiotherapist, Sue Matthews, could hardly get him to co-operate, and Michael spent some time with him reviewing his injuries and explaining the various stages of his rehabilitation. Even he gave up in the end.

'Said he should have broken his neck—today I'm inclined to agree with him,' he said in a rare moment of criticism. 'Ungrateful young fool—he doesn't seem to realise how lucky he's been. He should make a full recovery provided that tib and fib unite OK, and there's every chance they will. Really, I could hit him!'

'Unfortunately we don't have anyone worse off we can put him near—that often works wonders,' Mary O'Brien said sagely. 'Do you have time for a cup of coffee before you go back to Clinic, Michael?'

He shook his head. 'No, I should be up there now. God knows when I'll be out. I'm supposed to have the afternoon off but it's looking unlikely. I'll see you later, darling.'

He dropped a kiss on Clare's cheek, and left, his footsteps receding in the stunned silence.

'So that's the way of it,' Mary O'Brien said.

Clare's face softened in a smile. 'We're getting married as soon as we can sort out the date.'

Mary enveloped her in a motherly hug. 'That's wonderful, Clare! I'm delighted for you. He's a lovely, lovely man, and a brilliant surgeon. You'll make a beautiful couple. I hope you're very happy.'

Clare flushed. 'Thank you, Sister.' She glanced at her watch. 'Have I got time to do a teaching round with the third-years? I thought the management of Barry Warner's injuries would make quite an interesting topic.'

'Good idea, Clare. Might get him out of his stupor, all those lovely girls dancing attendance on him. I'll deal with the discharges.'

All too soon it was lunchtime, and then drugs again, and before she knew where she was Michael was back.

'You're finished!'

He nodded. 'We skipped lunch. What time are you off?'

'Four. Can you hang on? We need to go to the supermarket on the way home.'

He grimaced. 'Domestic bliss! OK, I'll hang on— any chance of a cup of tea?'

'Not unless you help yourself. We're all busy!'

At ten to four she popped her head round the office door. Michael was in there, his feet propped on a chair, laughing with Mary O'Brien.

'Nice to see everyone's comfortable!' she said with a chuckle.

Then the phone rang, and Clare watched in dismay as Mary's face became grave.

'Dear God! How many can we expect?'

Michael's feet dropped to the floor and he put down his cup.

'Yes, Michael Barrington's here, and Clare Stevens. They're both off-duty now—hang on, I'll ask them.' She covered the receiver, and looked up. 'Commuter train derailment. Apparently it's a hell of a mess. Several casualties trapped in the wreckage. They want a volunteer mobile surgical team on the scene for emergency amputations and on-the-spot immobilisation of spinal injuries. Can you go?'

They both nodded.

'Go down to A & E—Jim Harris is organising it. They want as many beds as we can spare—I'll get some of our long-stay cases shipped over to Medical for now. Off you go—and good luck!'

The Accident and Emergency department was in full swing. Non-urgent cases had been advised to go and see their GPs, urgent cases were being dealt with as quickly as possible. The more easily accessible casualties were already arriving from the scene of the crash, and they found Jim Harris in the staff room with a whiteboard, sketching in a flow-chart to show everyone their places.

Clare and Michael were attached to an anaesthetist, another nurse and an off-duty houseman from general surgery. They were to proceed to the scene of the crash and liaise with the incident medical officer and incident control officer.

It was horrendous. Even the most seasoned ambulance men and firemen were shocked by the carnage. The train had left the rails and plunged down an embankment, the third carriage riding up over the second. Most of the dead and injured had been in the second carriage, and those who were trapped by the wreckage were still in there, but the carriage towering over it was highly unstable, and the wind was picking up, rocking it with every gust. As a result they had to wait until the firemen had finished rigging up huge props to support the structure before they were allowed in.

Of the several people still trapped in the second carriage, only two were badly hurt; the others were quickly freed by the firemen and taken away after assessment, or were not trapped and were attended to by the houseman and the anaesthetist. Apart from minor crush injuries and a few fractures, most of the people were cut, bruised and simply terrified, and who could blame them?

Suppressing a shudder of horror, Clare went with Michael to examine the two trapped in the rear of the carriage. One, an elderly woman, was pinned to the floor by the crumpled rear wall of the carriage. She had serious chest injuries and was unlikely to survive. She was mercifully unconscious. The other, a man in his late twenties, was trapped by the foot and was clearly in great pain.

He gripped Clare's hand and hung on like grim death.

'Get me out of here,' he moaned, 'please, I can't stand it—get me out!'

Michael made a quick and thorough assessment of his injuries, and knelt by the man's head.

'Hello there. Can you tell me your name?'

'Alan,' he whispered harshly. 'Alan Beedale.'

'OK, Alan, I'm Michael. I'm an orthopaedic surgeon—I specialise in bones. Alan, I've had a look at your foot, and from what I can see it's very badly damaged.'

'Am I going to lose it?' he asked jerkily.

Michael nodded. 'I think that's quite likely. I'll talk

to the firemen and see if they can get you out in one
piece, but I think even if they can, your foot won't heal
now. The damage is too extensive. I'll get the anaesthetist to come and check you over, because either way,
we'll knock you out before we move you. OK?'

The man nodded weakly, and Clare wiped away the
sweat that was beading on his brow.

'Don't worry, Alan, they'll soon have you out of
here,' she murmured comfortingly.

The anaesthetist appeared at her side. 'Hello, old
son. Could I just have a listen to your chest?' After a
few seconds he nodded. 'Fine. When did you eat?'

'Lunch—twelve o'clock today—just a roll.'

'That's fine. Right, we'll soon have you more
comfortable. Can you get me a vein, Staff?' He drew
up the anaesthetic into a syringe, swabbed the vein
Clare had exposed and within seconds the man was
unconscious. 'Right, keep an eye on his blood-pressure
for me, will you? I'll get an airway in.'

Then Michael was back with the fireman.

'No way, mate,' he said with a shake of his head.
'The whole weight of the third carriage is resting on his
foot. We won't get him out without heavy lifting gear,
and that could take hours. Her, too.' He tipped his
head towards the elderly woman. 'Looks like she's a
gonner anyway.'

Michael nodded. 'OK. I rather thought it was a non-
starter. Thanks anyway. Right, Peter—can I begin?'

'Are you going to take his foot off?' Clare asked
quietly.

'No choice.'

'Oh, God, how awful! He's so young—his whole life
ahead of him, ruined—oh, Michael, isn't there any
way you can avoid it?'

'You heard what the fireman said, Clare. It'll be hours before the lifting gear can shift that carriage, and by that time the circulation will have been cut off for so long he'll lose his foot anyway, and probably half his leg with it.'

'But he'll be crippled!' she whispered.

'That's the way the cookie crumbles. Are you going to help me, or just get in the way?' Michael snapped.

She drew in a sharp breath. 'Sorry. Of course I'll help.'

He quickly covered the area with sterile paper sheets, cut away the man's trousers to expose the leg, and opened the surgical pack. The other nurse swabbed the area as thoroughly as possible given the limited access, and then swabbed Clare's and Michael's hands prior to them putting on their gloves.

'OK, chaps. Is he all right, Peter?'

'Fine,' the anaesthetist said. 'Help yourself.'

'I'm going to do a guillotine amputation—access is bloody difficult. They can sort him out in Theatre when they get him back. Scalpel, please.'

Clare fought down her feelings of distress and forced herself to be professional as she watched his systematic dissection of the soft tissues. She closed her eyes at the high-pitched whine of the power saw, and then it was over, the man was freed from the wreckage and the ambulance team was waiting to take him to hospital.

That left only the elderly woman with the chest injuries.

A sudden gust of wind shook the train, and a fireman stuck his head in through the opening in the side. 'You'd better get out, mate—this lot's going to go in a minute, the props aren't holding.'

'I can't leave this woman,' Michael said.

'You're a bloody fool, my friend. If that carriage comes down, it'll take you with it. She's a gonner anyway.'

Clare tugged at his arm, chill fingers of fear crawling up her spine. 'Please, Michael—there's nothing you can do for her!'

'Yes, there is. I can stay with her until she dies. You get out and wait for me. It won't be long. I'll give her an injection if she comes round. Go on, love. I don't want you in here.'

'I'm not leaving you——'

'Do as you're told, Clare. I don't have time to worry about you now.'

'I'll wait here.' She retreated to the other end of the carriage and perched herself in a corner, watching him and listening to his soft voice as he crouched under the twisted metal by the dying woman.

Each time the wind gusted, Clare's heart hammered louder in her throat as she watched the man she loved in his selfless vigil.

At one point the woman must have regained consciousness, because his voice became more directed, and he gave her an injection—probably diamorphine.

Then, after an age, he lifted his head. 'OK, she's gone. Come on, Clare, let's get out.'

Just then there was a huge gust of wind, and with a scream of tortured metal, the carriage above collapsed.

'Clare, get out——!'

His voice was cut off abruptly and Clare watched in horror as the roof of the carriage buckled and crumpled like a paper bag.

'Michael!'

She heard a ragged groan, and crawled up the carriage towards him. It was tilted at a crazy angle, and she could see him, lying flat out, one leg bent up, trying to drag himself forwards.

'Are you all right?' she asked him desperately.

'My leg,' he groaned. 'I think it's caught—damn. Clare, get out.'

'No way.' She crawled the rest of the way and grabbed his hand, and he gripped it like a lifeline. Lifting herself up, she peered over his shoulder and clamped her lips shut on the scream of horror.

Where his left foot had been was a huge block of twisted metal.

'Can you see?' he whispered.

She nodded. 'The firemen will have to free you,' she said in an astonishingly calm voice. 'I'll get them.'

They were already behind her, assessing the situation and muttering in hurried undertones.

She didn't need to hear what they were saying. The gnarled lump of contorted metal was part of the third carriage, and it wasn't going anywhere. In a cruel twist of fate, Michael was trapped, and there was only one way out.

Peter was by her side in an instant, taking in the scene with eyes that missed nothing.

'How does it look?' Michael asked, his face white with pain.

'Not good, old chap. It's your left leg——'

'I know what it is, I can feel the damn thing,' he gritted. 'Does it need to come off?'

'Dear God, no, not Michael!' Clare sobbed.

Peter pursed his lips and nodded. 'I would say so.'

'No!' she screamed. 'No, you can't!'

'Do it,' he muttered. 'And get Clare out of here.'

Peter was already drawing up the anaesthetic. The other nurse was as near as she could get to the end of

the carriage, and Ross Hamilton appeared as if by
magic and took charge. The wind gusted again, and the
carriage shifted. Michael flung his head back in agony,
and Peter found a vein in his outstretched hand and
sent him to merciful oblivion.

'Out, Clare, you don't want to see this.'

'I can't leave him,' she whispered.

'Have it your own way,' Peter said with a sigh, and
turned back to Ross.

'OK, he's yours.'

Dry-eyed, Clare watched as they stripped away his
trouser leg to reveal the damage. Ross swore quietly,
then his voice assumed a cold professional tone, as if
he was delivering a lecture.

'Extensive de-gloving, nerve and major vessel
damage, severe comminution of the tib and fib. We
wouldn't save it anyway. OK, everyone. Let's just get
him out fast and back to Theatre. Mayhew can tidy
him up.'

He picked up a scalpel and neatly stripped the soft
tissues away from the bone, then he reached for the
saw. Clare turned and fled.

It was three hours before he came down from
Recovery. Mary O'Brien was still on, and after one
look at Clare she sent her home to shower and change.

The cottage seemed appallingly empty without him.
She fed O'Malley, and went up to the bathroom to
shower. Wrapped in her towel, she wandered into the
bedroom and stumbled over Michael's shoes.

It was only then that it really hit her, and with a little
cry she collapsed on the bed, huge dry sobs tearing at
her throat. His scent was on the sheets, making him so
real she could almost feel his presence. One by one the

heavy tears started to fall, becoming a flood that spent finally itself, leaving her exhausted but calm.

She dressed in uniform, knowing that they would be rushed off their feet and that every hand would be needed. Michael, for one, would need specialling for the first twenty-four hours at least, and there would be others.

She was back on the ward before Michael, and busied herself with settling in the new patients, her nerves at breaking point.

When he appeared she was shocked at his pallor.

God knows I shouldn't be, she thought, I've seen this sort of thing often enough, but somehow, when it's someone you love——

Tim Mayhew was with him, and he beckoned to her.

She went with him into the little side-ward opposite the nursing station, and stared numbly at Michael as they transferred his motionless body to the bed.

'How is he?' she asked through stiff lips.

'He'll be all right. The damage lower down was appalling, I gather, but I've been able to leave him with an excellent stump, thank God. He'll be up and about in no time.'

She nodded. 'Just so long as he's alive. . .'

Tim Mayhew patted her on the arm. 'It's a terrible blow, so soon after your engagement. It'll take a very special person to cope with him, Clare. Don't take it on if you don't feel you can stick at it.'

'I love him,' she said tonelessly. 'We'll manage.'

Mary O'Brien bustled in. 'You'll be no use to me anywhere else on the ward, with your mind in here with him, and he's in no position to object—would you like to special him for me, Clare?'

They elevated the foot of the bed to encourage the

venous return from the stump, and then Mary left her alone with him.

He kept her busy. Every fifteen minutes she took his temperature, pulse and respiration, and his blood-pressure, and he was linked to a cardiac monitor and a Pethidine pump for continuous pain relief. The last unit of whole blood was running in, and after that there was the saline infusion to set up, and drugs to inject into the giving set.

When he woke he was very disorientated, unable to remember anything and extremely agitated by the drip. The third time he tried to tear it out she called for help and David Blake, the junior registrar, gave him a sedative. After that things were easier for a while, but as the night wore on and the sedative wore off he began to stir again.

Clare, anticipating trouble, immediately began to talk to him soothingly. To her surprise his eyes opened and he looked straight at her.

'God, I hurt,' he whispered. 'What happened?'

She was cautious. 'What do you remember?'

'We were somewhere—a train? Derailment. Old lady dying—oh, God.'

She watched his face as recollection came. His eyes fluttered closed and he swallowed.

'Did they take my leg off?'

'Yes.'

He swore succinctly. 'Where?'

'Below the knee. They had no choice, Michael.'

'Who did it?'

She closed her eyes against the memory. 'Ross Hamilton. He was marvellous. Then Tim Mayhew took over when they got you back here——' Her voice cracked.

Michael reached out his hand and groped for hers. Their fingers linked and clung.

'I'm sorry,' he whispered. 'I couldn't leave her alone. No one should die alone. I'm sorry, Clare.'

She bit her lips and fought back the tears. After a few minutes his fingers relaxed as he slipped back into sleep, and she checked his TPR and filled in his chart again, then made herself look at the stump dressing to check for signs of bleeding. There was none, and the suction drain had produced only a small quantity of almost clear serum.

Medically speaking, he was doing very well. Exhausted, Clare rested her cheek against the cool glass of the window pane and sighed. How would they cope? How would *he* cope?

He always advocated amputation and rapid rehabilitation after drastic trauma, in preference to more conservative treatment—now he would see what it was like with the boot on the other foot, so to speak, she thought with bitter irony.

She closed her eyes against the weary tears. God, she was so tired. She heard the door open and close softly, and prised herself away from the window.

It was Ross Hamilton, still in Theatre greens, his face grey with exhaustion. 'How is he?' he asked, his soft Scots burr reassuring in the lonely night.

'Clinically excellent,' she told him, trying desperately to keep the wobble out of her voice.

'Poor wee lassie,' he said gently, and, opening his arms, he folded her against his chest.

'I can't bear it, Ross,' she sobbed. 'I hate to see him like this. He's so strong, so fit—it doesn't seem right! I just feel I can't help him.'

'You can, you can help him a great deal, but not like

this. Why don't you go and have a cup of tea and half an hour's kip? I'll sit with him for a wee while. Go on.'

'But he might wake up and want me—and his obs need doing——'

'You don't think I can manage that?' he said with heavy irony. 'Go on, lass. Go and lie down. You're no good to him like that.'

She made a cup of tea and curled up in the day-room under a blanket, sure she wouldn't sleep, but she did, for almost two hours, before Judith Price woke her.

'He's awake and asking for you,' she said gently.

'Oh—what's the time? Oh, no! I'm supposed to be specialling him——'

'Don't worry, my staff nurse has been doing it for the last hour and a half. Mr Hamilton went home—he said to leave you. Don't worry, love, Michael's fine. He's slept well, and he's quite alert now. Have a little wash and comb your hair, and I'll tell him you'll be in in a minute.'

She looked a fright, of course. She snatched off her cap, finger-combed her hair into some sort of order and scraped it back up on top, pinning it ruthlessly before fixing her cap on top of the chaos. Her face looked pale and worried, and she practised a cheery smile that made her want to weep.

Hurrying back along the corridor, she could hear the ward beginning to stir as dawn heralded the end of another long and, for many, sleepless night.

He was lying on his back, his face turned towards the door, and as she went in he reached out his hand towards her.

'I'm sorry, I should have been here when you woke up——'

'It's OK. My poor darling—has it been a hell of a night?'

'Pretty ghastly, but not a patch on yours. How are you feeling?'

'Wrung out. My leg aches like the very devil, but I suppose it would. I haven't looked at it yet.'

She was silent. That would be the hardest part, in many ways, of course. After that there would be no fooling himself, no pretending it was all a dream.

'Help me up,' he muttered.

'What?'

'I said help me up. I want to look.'

'Michael——'

His glare silenced her. With a helpless shrug she put her arm round him and helped him to raise his shoulders off the bed.

He didn't say anything, just stared at his stump for a long time and then nodded.

'I wondered if it was a dream,' he said with a wry smile. 'I knew it was all too good to be true.'

He lay back against the pillows, exhausted by the effort, and he seemed to sleep for a while.

Just before eight Tim Mayhew came to see him again, and Clare left them alone together for a while. Mary O'Brien appeared at eight, and found Clare in the office, sipping coffee and staring out of the window.

'Gracious, child, are you still here? How is the boy?'

'Just as you'd expect—taking it on the chin. Mr Mayhew's with him now. It's been a fairly grim night on the ward, by all accounts.'

Mary nodded. 'Everyone's very shocked. They're all terribly upset about Michael. It seems that the only women staff in the hospital who aren't in love with him are either married or old enough to be his mother—

and not all of them are as immune as they should be!
And the men are all very shaken. It would appear that
in the short time he's been here he's earned a great
deal of respect from his colleagues.'

Clare felt a huge lump in her throat, and swallowed
to shift it.

'Ah, love, come on now. Why don't you go home to
bed?'

His bed? With his scent on the sheets and his shoes
lying all around to trip her up? Oh, no.

She shuddered. 'I'm fine. He might need me. I had
a few hours' sleep in the night.'

'Less than two,' said Sister Price, coming in. 'Mr
Mayhew would like to speak to you in Mr Barrington's
room, Staff.'

'Thanks.' She put down her coffee, slipped her shoes
back on and made her way over to the side-ward.

Tim Mayhew stood up as she went in and gave her a
smile. 'Hello, there. He's doing well, isn't he? Did he
have a good night?'

'Reasonably good, I think. He was a little restless at
about ten and had a sedative, but after that he was
fine.'

'Good. Well, the heart monitor is obviously
unnecessary, so that can come off, and I think we can
cut out the quarter-hourly obs and bring it down to
half-hourly, then hourly if he's stable by this evening.
Try him on some fluids—water to start with, then fruit
juice, squash, mineral water—see how he tolerates it.
If it's OK, then maybe a light supper?'

'Yuck,' Michael commented weakly.

'Yuck nothing,' Clare told him. 'Shall I get you some
Perrier?'

'Yes, there's tons in the fridge. While you're there, can you feed O'Malley?'

'Did it last night.'

'Thanks.' His voice faded to a thread, and his eyes drifted shut. Mr Mayhew beckoned her to the door.

'He's doing very well. If this continues we'll get the physiotherapist on him later today and as soon as that drain comes out he can start walking—we'll get him down to Physio on a pneumatic leg so he doesn't forget how to walk, and then the people from the Limb Centre can take the cast on Tuesday week—they're coming in anyway for the electives.'

She nodded. 'How's Alan Beedale?'

'The amputee from the train crash? Pretty grim. He's in ITU at the moment—probably be up here tomorrow. He'd lost a lot of blood and was very shocked, and he's got other injuries as well. By all accounts young Barrington was very lucky.'

'You think so?' Clare said sadly. 'I can't help seeing him as he was on Thursday, windsurfing—so graceful, so strong, so free—he's lost all that, and I don't know how he'll take it.'

'Well, windsurfing will be a bit tricky, but I have heard of amputees who've done it—need a special leg, of course, but certainly he'll be able to sail his boat without too much difficulty. I think the problem will be holding him back, not getting him going. Let's wait and see, eh? There's a lot of water to go under a great many bridges before we have to worry about that.'

Deborah Lewis came out of Sister's office then, and her shocked eyes met Clare's in a message of silent sympathy.

'How is he?' she asked.

Clare shrugged. 'Doing very well. He's asleep at the moment.'

Deborah nodded. 'I'm specialling him this morning—why don't you go home and rest while he's asleep?'

'Why is everybody trying to get me to go home?' she asked frantically. 'I don't *want* to be at home, I want to be *here*, where I can see that he's all right——'

'And he can see that you aren't,' Mary O'Brien said firmly, appearing at Clare's elbow and steering her into her office. 'You need to go and have a long, hot bath, get your head down for a few hours and come back when you can be of some use to him. Like this you're no good to anybody. Now, can you drive, or do you want someone to take you?'

Clare shook her head. 'I'll be fine. I'm sorry, I know you're right. I'll just go and tell him what I'm doing.'

But he was asleep. She stood looking down at him for several minutes, noting almost absently that his colour had returned, that his breathing was deep and regular, that the pulse in his throat was slow and steady and strong. If she didn't look at his leg, she could almost believe. . .

'Goodness, that was a deep sigh, Clare,' Deborah teased gently. 'Go on, I'll take care of your precious man for you. He'll probably sleep for hours.'

She made her way to the car, and drove home almost mechanically. O'Malley greeted her ecstatically, winding round her legs and yowling for attention.

She lifted him up and draped him round her neck, where he lay contentedly while she made herself a drink and took it in the garden. The sun was warm, not yet hot, and she lifted her face to it and tried to banish the horror of the night. O'Malley slithered down into her lap and lay against her chest, his claws kneading her shoulder rhythmically in time to his purring.

'That hurts, O'Malley,' she complained gently, detaching his claws, and with an offended squawk he jumped off her lap and flowed under the nearest bush, tail twitching.

She ran a hot bath and fell asleep in it, waking when it was cold to the ringing of the phone. It was her mother.

'Hello, darling,' she said brightly. 'I tried to get you last night but you must have been out. Did you have a lovely time?'

'Oh, God, Mummy,' she said, her voice breaking, and for several minutes she could say nothing. Her mother let her cry, and then, when she recovered a little, questioned her gently.

When Clare told her what had happened, there was a shocked silence for a few seconds and then she managed to find her voice. 'Would you like me to come over?'

'I'm going to the hospital to see him in a minute. You could meet me there. I don't know if he'll be up to having visitors—oh, lord, Mum, I'll have to tell his grandfather and his parents. I don't think I can cope!'

'Clare, listen to me. Just calm down. Go to the hospital, and we'll see you there as soon as we can make it. It shouldn't take more than an hour from Cambridge. Don't worry about anything else. Just take it one step at a time.'

They didn't speak for much longer. There didn't seem a great deal to say.

After she put the phone down and got dressed, Clare found various bottles of mineral water, Coke and so on in the fridge, and put them in the car, together with some clean boxer shorts and a couple of loose-fitting short-sleeved shirts. There were no pyjamas that she could see. She also packed his wash-things, his after-shave and a couple of books that he had been meaning to read and not got round to.

When she arrived back at the hospital, he was awake and sitting propped up slightly in bed, staring at the window. He turned towards her and his eyes lit up.

'Clare—are you OK?'

'I'm fine,' she managed to say, but had to look away so he wouldn't see the misery in her eyes. 'How are you doing?' She busied herself with his chart.

'Hey, leave that alone, you're off duty. What's in the bag?'

'Wash-things, drinks, some boxer shorts and shirts—don't you have any pyjamas?'

He chuckled wearily. 'What would I do with pyjamas? Come here.'

He patted the sheet beside him and she perched on the edge of the bed and unpacked the bag, laying the things out on the top of his locker.

'I brought you those books——'

'Clare?'

'Would you like a drink? Let me pour you——'

'Clare! Stop fiddling with those things and look at me.'

She stopped, winding her hands into the plastic of the carrier bag to stop them trembling.

His hand came up and turned her face round towards him. 'That's better,' he said softly, searching her face. 'How about a kiss?'

'Oh, Michael——'

She turned away, unable to stop the tears.

'Oh, God, please don't cry. I don't think I can be brave for both of us, love.'

'I'm sorry. . .' She snatched a tissue off the locker and scrubbed furiously at her face.

'Smile for me?'

She gave him a wobbly smile.

'You know what? I could do with a hug,' he said, his voice choked, and she laid her head against his chest and wrapped her arms around him, reassured by the steady beat of his heart.

One step at a time, her mother said.

Dear God, it was going to be harder, far harder, than she had imagined.

CHAPTER FIVE

DEBORAH LEWIS had slipped out when Clare arrived, to give them a little privacy, but after a few minutes she came back in.

Clare lifted her head and eased her arms away from Michael's shoulders. He was asleep again, his hair tousled, and he looked suddenly very young and vulnerable.

Deborah's mouth tightened in sympathy. She took his pulse, counted his breathing and then slipped the thermometer under his tongue. He didn't stir, either then or when she inflated the cuff of the sphygmomanometer to check his blood-pressure.

'OK?' Clare asked softly. Deborah nodded.

'Mr Mayhew's on the ward—he's coming to have a look at the stump in a minute. How's he going on fluids?'

She checked the level of the water jug, jotted the amount on the chart and returned the board to the end of the bed just as Tim Mayhew came in.

'Ah, Clare, my dear—out of uniform at last. How is the patient?' he asked, skimming the charts.

'Sleeping a lot. I think it's sinking in.'

He nodded slowly. 'Yes, that is always the hardest part with a traumatic amputation. The next hurdle is getting him to look at it without a dressing—which is what I want to do now. Are you staying, or going?'

She met his sympathetic eyes. 'May I stay?'

'Of course. I imagine you'll be partly responsible for

his nursing care in the next couple of weeks anyway, so you'll see it sooner or later. Might as well get it over with.'

Mary O'Brien wheeled in a dressing trolley, and while Deborah supported his leg, Mary unwrapped the light crêpe bandage and removed the wadding.

Summoning up her professionalism, Clare forced herself to watch. He had done a neat job, she had to give him that. There was a suture line running diagonally across the end of his stump, the sutures alternating with Steristrips to avoid scarring.

'I did a skew-flap myoplastic amputation, which is what he himself would have chosen, of course, partly because it's best cosmetically and surgically, and partly because the recovery time is quickest and, knowing Michael, he'll want to be up and about in the shortest possible time. Yes, that looks very healthy. Of course the tissues were quite undamaged at this level so we've got optimum conditions—a fit, healthy patient, a clean limb, little delay before operation—really one couldn't ask for more. The other chap's in much worse shape.'

He inspected the fluid collected by the suction drain, nodded his satisfaction and asked Mary O'Brien to redress the wound. 'How's he coping with the pain?'

'He's been getting a bit edgy,' Deborah said. 'He hasn't complained, but he's obviously in quite a lot of pain.'

'Hmm. Well, we'll leave it as it is if we can, but I'll write him up for more in case you think he needs it. There's nothing to be gained from unnecesary suffering. Right, thank you, ladies. I'll be back later today to see how he is.'

As the door closed behind him, Mary O'Brien looked up from the dressing.

'OK?'

Clare nodded. 'Yes, I think so. It's all a bit unreal.'

Mary smiled understandingly. 'I'm sure. Your mother and father are here, my love. I've put them in the day-room. Why don't you take them for a cup of coffee?'

She did that, and told them in detail all about the horrendous events of the past twenty-four hours. Somehow talking about it helped to get it in perspective, and they were philosophical and supportive, but naturally worried about Clare.

'It's such a new relationship, darling,' her mother said gently, 'and I just wonder if you'll find it has the strength to come through. In many ways it might be best if it doesn't——'

'Mummy! I love him—how could it possibly be best?'

Her father laid a soothing hand on her shoulder. 'I think what your mother is saying is that you should keep an eye on your feelings—don't let them cloud your judgement, and above all, don't stay with him out of pity. You'll have to keep your sympathy firmly under wraps, I would imagine—he didn't strike me as a man who takes kindly to molly-coddling.'

She nodded. 'I'll bear it in mind—and I will have to keep my own feelings away from him, I know that. I must get back to him. Thank you so much for coming over, I feel much better. I'll ring you tonight.'

She kissed them goodbye at the main entrance and made her way back to the ward just as Michael woke up.

'Perfect timing,' Deborah said. 'You can take over and do his pressure areas while I go for lunch—bye, gorgeous. Be good, now!'

He gave a tired laugh and lifted a hand in a weary wave.

Clare smiled. 'How are you feeling?'

'Sore—Deborah's just increased the Pethidine. Do I really have to have another bloody back-rub?'

'I don't know, some people are so ungrateful,' she scolded cheerfully. 'Come on, let's have you over on your side—carefully does it—that's lovely.' As she powdered her hand and rubbed firmly over the base of his spine, he sighed and seemed to resign himself to the treatment. After she had finished his shoulders and elbows, she moved to his heel.

'Well, at least I'm saving you some time at that end,' he said drily.

'Oh, God, Michael. . .'

'Sorry, that was a sick joke,' he apologised gruffly. 'Thank you, that's much better.'

'How about a wash and a shave?'

'I'm tempted. I feel filthy.'

She blanket-bathed him, helped him shave and clean his teeth, and then straightened his pillows and changed the draw sheet. 'I expect they'll get you out of bed tomorrow,' she said cheerfully. 'That'll be something to look forward to.'

'Clare, the only thing I'm looking forward to is getting out of here and back on my feet—oh, hell. You know what I mean.'

She nodded, her throat too tight to speak.

'I wonder when it will be?'

'One day at a time, eh, soldier? Let's get today over with first. Have you got any Perrier yet?'

'No, I'd love some. Trouble is, the more I drink, the more I want to pee.'

She shrugged and handed him a glass of mineral

water. 'That's fine. You have to keep your system going. Just thank your lucky stars you didn't have to have a catheter!'

'It's a small consolation!' He grimaced. 'It's all so bloody public!'

'You wait till you need the commode!'

Michael snorted. 'I shall wait until I'm up on crutches, or die in the attempt. God, Clare, I never realised how humiliating it is lying in bed dependent on someone else for your very functions!'

She squeezed his hand. 'It's only me, Michael.'

'That's worse.' His eyes as they met hers were inexpressibly sad. 'You shouldn't have to see all this. It isn't fair on you.'

She was silent for a long time, and then she looked away. 'Tough. Just try getting rid of me.'

She went out with the dirty linen, took a deep breath to steady herself and went back into the room. At first she thought he was asleep, but he opened his eyes and looked at her, then gave her a travesty of a smile.

'You're a good girl,' he said softly. 'I'm sorry this had to happen.'

She shrugged and sighed. 'Just get better, eh?' she said in a choked voice. 'Now, is there anything else I can do for you?'

Physically, he progressed rapidly. By Monday morning the suction drain was out and he was up on crutches with support, and mid-morning saw him down in the Physiotherapy department walking between parallel bars with a pneumatic limb. The structure, carefully designed to encase the whole limb in inflated bags supported by a metal frame, was designed for use very early on to get amputees up and about before they forgot how to walk. It helped to overcome the problem of contractures in the limb caused by the change in muscle balance, and getting patients back on their feet quickly was good for morale.

Not that Michael's morale was noticeably low. By Tuesday he was practising in his room on crutches, and by Wednesday he was emerging from his doorway to chat to the other patients.

It was on Wednesday morning that Clare, dealing with Danny Drew in one of his most ebullient moods, began to realise that Michael was actually very depressed.

Danny looked over her head and said loudly, 'Hey, lads, it's lover-boy. How d'you lose your leg, mate? Bit careless, wasn't it?'

Michael gave him a knowing smile and raised a crutch in a salute. 'Morning, Danny. Still on form, I see. Never mind, they'll have you down to Physio soon. You'll enjoy that. Bit of pain and frustration will make a man of you yet.'

Then he turned awkwardly on his heel and worked his way back to his room.

'How dare you speak to him like that?' Clare said with quiet savagery. 'Shall I tell you how he lost his leg? An old lady was dying, and he refused to leave her alone, so he was trapped when the train collapsed. I wonder if you would have had that much courage?'

She snapped the sheet back over him, turned on her heel and followed Michael back into his room.

'Are you OK? Bloody little fool, I could kill him!'

He was standing by the window, staring out across the woodland beside the hospital.

'I'll survive,' he said with dry irony. 'Actually I could do with some privacy, Clare, if you don't mind.'

She drew in a sharp breath, stunned by his rejection. 'Sorry. I—of course.'

She went into Sister's office and slumped down at the desk. She had sensed his withdrawal from her for some days, but this was the first time he had actually told her to leave him alone.

Shaking off her misery—after all, no one liked to be rejected—she busied herself with the details of ward administration that had to be dealt with that morning.

It was no good, she couldn't concentrate. She knew he had phoned his grandfather on a couple of occasions—she also knew that he hadn't told him about his leg. His parents were abroad on holiday and wouldn't be back for some weeks, and as he said, there was no point in telling them. He had phoned his brother, though, in Germany, and told him. He had also told him not to come, but Clare thought it was a mistake. He had no one except her to lean on, and he didn't seem inclined to lean on her at all, rather sheltering her from his pain and frustration.

How could you help a man who wouldn't let you?

She would just have to get him out. At lunchtime she went into his room and suggested he join the other mobile patients in the ward at the long table in the day-room.

'No, thank you. I'll eat in here.'

'Michael, I think——'

'Clare, lay off! I don't want to go out there and be jolly!'

'I wasn't suggesting you did,' she said quietly. 'I just thought some company might do you good.'

'I don't want their company,' he said bitterly. 'I'm not interested in their curious sympathy or their damned haemorrhoids!'

She stood her ground. 'How about eating with Barry Warner, then? He can't get out and he's very fed up.'

She saw a flicker of guilt. 'How is he? I haven't even asked.'

'Oh, he's making quite good progress physically, but he's very uncomfortable and extremely introverted. He can't hold a book, he says the telly's awful——'

'I have to agree with him,' Michael said wryly. 'OK, I'll have lunch with Barry—this time.'

He wheeled round and worked his way up the ward to Barry's door, knocking lightly before opening it and going in.

'How's the patient today?' he said cheerfully.

'Foul—bloody hell, what happened to you?'

Clare left him with his explanations, and asked the ward orderly to deliver their meals to Barry's room. Some time later she heard laughter coming from the room, and sighed with relief. Perhaps now he would be all right.

But she was over-optimistic. By mid-afternoon he was back in his room, lying on his bed staring blankly out of the window.

She was off-duty at four, and went in to sit with him.

He glanced disinterestedly at her and then returned to his contemplation of the window.

'Don't you have something to do? Drugs to give, notes to write, rotas to juggle?'

'I'm off-duty,' she told him. 'I thought you might appreciate a visitor.'

'The only person I really want to see is Pop,' he said bluntly, 'and I just can't face telling him——'

His voice cracked and he turned his head away.

'Oh, darling,' she murmured and took his hand. It

lay unresponsive in hers, and after a few seconds she squeezed it and let go, standing up.

'Would you like me to tell him?'

He looked back at her, his eyes tortured. 'Would you? It's a lot to ask. I'd love to see him.'

'I'll bring him in tonight.'

'Thanks.'

She bent her head to kiss him, but at the last second he turned away and her lips brushed his cheek.

She breathed in sharply, unbearably hurt. 'I'll see you later,' she said, as evenly as she could manage, and fled before she disgraced herself by bursting into tears.

Pop took it very well, considering. He sat in his chair in the garden, his gnarled hands knotted on the top of his cane, and stared into the distance for some minutes. Then with a heavy sigh, he turned to Clare.

'I knew there was something wrong when he rang me. Something about his voice. That's the thing about being blind, your ears take over. I didn't like to ask— never do. The boy'll tell me most things in good time, and if he doesn't—well, I've learn to control my curiosity. But this. . .' He shook his head sadly. 'So how is he?'

'Physically excellent. He's made tremendous progress and is walking on a special inflated limb in the Physio department, and he's learning to manage his crutches very well. He doesn't seem to be in pain any more, but. . .'

Pop waited, giving her time.

'He's very withdrawn. I think he's trying to protect me or something, but he won't lean on me so I feel I can't help him as much as I'd like. He needs you, Pop.'

He reached out a worn old hand and she took it,

drawing comfort from the reassuring squeeze. 'Needs you, too, but I doubt he'll admit it yet. Give him time, Clare. He's a proud man. He'll come round.' He levered himself to his feet and straightened slowly. 'Suppose we'd better go and see him, then. Can you give me a few minutes to get ready?'

'Of course—can I help?'

He snorted. 'Think I can still manage the bathroom on my own, my dear!' he said with a chuckle.

Clare smiled. 'Yes, I imagine you can, Pop. I'll wait for you out here. Call me when you're ready.'

When he appeared she helped him into her little car and drove back to the hospital, parking as close as she could to save his legs. Then she led him up to the ward.

Mary O'Brien was just coming out of Michael's room, and smiled at them. 'You've got a visitor, Michael!' she said brightly.

'Pop!' Michael turned from his position by the window and swung over to them on his crutches, his face working with emotion. 'It's good to see you!' His voice was unsteady.

'Hello, old son,' Pop said gruffly. 'Heard you were in the wars again.'

Michael sagged on to the edge of the bed and shot Clare a bleak look.

'Would you mind leaving us on our own?' he asked distantly.

'No, of course not. Here, Pop, sit yourself down on this chair—that's it. Would you like some tea?'

'No, thank you,' Michael said emphatically, and with a brief nod she left them alone.

She waited in Sister's office, watching through the open door. After nearly an hour the door of Michael's room opened and he stuck his head out.

'He's ready to go now,' he told her, and disappeared back inside.

She followed him into the room. His grandfather was still sitting on the chair, his face stony.

'Hello, Pop,' she said kindly. 'Ready for off?'

'Give me a hand up,' he demanded querulously.

She glanced at Michael but he looked away, so with a tiny shrug she took Pop's arm and helped him to his feet.

He paused at the door and turned. 'You're a bloody fool, son.'

'Bloody fool or not, Pop, it's my future, and I have a right to some say in it.'

'I think it's a grave mistake.'

'So it might be, but I don't think so,' Michael said heavily, and turned away.

'Goodnight,' said Clare quietly, but he ignored her.

The drive back was tense and fraught, each of them preoccupied with their thoughts. Clare was worried about Michael, and about the sudden gulf that seemed to have opened up between them. What had she said or done? Nothing that she could think of, but he was treating her like a leper—or was it himself he was treating like a leper? God knows, she thought. And what about Pop's parting shot? What was all that about?

Pop was obviously upset by his visit to Michael, but Clare already know him well enough to know he would tell her anything he wanted her to know. In his own words, she'd have to learn to control her curiosity.

She declined his offer of a drink, as it was already getting late and she had a long drive back to the cottage. It was dark by the time she turned into the gate, and was surprised to see a light on in the kitchen.

'How odd,' she said to herself. 'I must have left it on last night.'

Letting herself in without any thought of an intruder, she went straight into the kitchen as usual, and jerked instantly to a halt.

Michael was sitting sprawled in his usual place in the carver at the end of the table, and with a friendly smile he ambled to his feet and strolled towards her, his tanned, hair-strewn legs naked beneath old, comfortable shorts.

Her hand flew to her throat and her eyes widened in confusion.

'Michael. . .?'

'Sorry to startle you—we haven't met. I'm Andrew, Michael's brother. And you must be Clare.'

She couldn't take her eyes off his legs. They were just like Michael's—literally identical. Except for one detail.

They were perfect.

Clare didn't even realise she was crying until Andrew tipped up her chin and wiped her eyes with a soft, immaculately laundered handkerchief.

'Hey, I'm sorry. Did I give you a fright? I didn't realise you were living here until I broke in.'

'I—it isn't that.' She sniffed and he handed her the handkerchief.

'Be my guest!' he said in Michael's voice, and she bit down the sob.

After a few seconds she pulled herself together and blew her nose hard, pocketing the handkerchief.

'I—I'm sorry. It's just that I didn't realise—you're so like him, it was a bit of a shock. He didn't tell me. . .'

'That we're clones?' He gave a short, slightly bitter

laugh. 'No, it's a fact he normally tries to escape from. He's spent his life trying to be different, and I've copied him in everything, just to annoy him, but I guess he's won this time,' he said with heavy irony. 'Can I get you a drink?'

She noticed that there was an open bottle of wine on the table, half finished, and another empty on the worktop.

'Don't frown disapprovingly. I'm sure lover-boy won't mind.'

'No, I'm sure he won't, but you've had rather a lot, and presumably you have to drive to your hotel for the night——'

'What hotel? There's a spare room here, surely it won't worry you if I kip down in it?'

Clare sighed. This was Michael's twin brother, after all. She could hardly turn him away. 'Of course not. And yes, I will have a drink. Thank you.'

O'Malley came in and wound round her legs, then with a little yowl he leapt on to the worktop and up again on to her shoulders, draping himself round her neck.

'Hello, rascal,' she said, dropping gratefully into a chair, and he greeted her with a trembling squawk in her ear.

'Nice little place he's got here,' Andrew said with an expansive wave of his hand. His red wine slopped over the edge of the glass and dribbled on to the floor.

Clare got up and mopped it.

'What a domesticated little thing you are,' Andrew slurred.

'Not at all,' Clare told him repressively, 'but red wine stains the bricks.'

He stared at the floor for a moment and then back

at Clare. 'Sorry. So, Clare, tell me about my little brother—how is he?'

'To be honest, I'm not sure. Physically fine, mentally—I don't know how well he's coping. He's shut himself off from me——'

'Oh, join the club. That's why I didn't rush over—knew he wouldn't appreciate it. He's always been reclusive—I suppose that's why he gets on so well with the damn cat—they both go off to lick their wounds.'

'Except he can't.'

'Not yet, maybe, but he will, just as soon as he can. Me, I want all the sympathy and company I can get!'

Clare laughed, despite herself. Andrew was all right, and he couldn't help looking like Michael. Although, as she was beginning to realise, the resemblance was only physical. Michael was just as open and direct on the surface—whereas she rather thought that Andrew was all surface, with none of Michael's quiet, still depths. Perhaps she was doing him an injustice.

'Would you mind very much if I deprive you of my sympathy and company tonight? It's been a long day and I have to be at work by eight.'

He raised his glass. 'Be my guest. Goodnight, sweet Clare. Sleep well—and get up quietly, eh?'

She gave him a level look. 'I always do.'

'Wonderful. Adieu, fair maid. . .'

She left him, slouched against the table, his glass dangling from his fingers. He was going to have a hell of a head in the morning.

In fact he was up and about by seven, with no obvious signs of the previous night's excesses.

'Seen the Porsche?' he greeted Clare, coming in through the back door as she came down the stairs.

'Good morning, Andrew. No, I imagine it must still be at the hospital where Michael left it on Friday. Why?'

'Well, obviously he doesn't have any further use for it, so I thought I'd have it back,' he said with a shrug.

'Fine—how did you get here yesterday, by the way?'

'Taxi,' he said economically.

'Oh—right. I'll give you a lift in. Did you make coffee?'

'Sorry. I put the kettle on but that's as far as I got. Do you suppose I could see him this morning, or do I have to wait for visiting?'

Clare put two cups on the worktop and turned towards Andrew. It still hurt her in a way to look at him, to look into those startling blue eyes so frankly assessing her. 'No, we have open visiting. You can see him at any time. Why don't you come in with me in a minute?'

'OK. Is that coffee for me?'

'Yes. Andrew, do you mind if I say something?'

He shot her a keen look. 'No, of course not. What is it?'

Clare took a deep breath. 'Do you think you could cover up your legs?'

He gave a short laugh and his eyes travelled over her with undisguised interest. 'Why? Are they upsetting you, my love?'

Oh, God, she thought, he even calls me the same thing. 'No, not really, but they may well upset Michael.'

He sobered instantly. 'Hell, I hadn't thought. Yes, I'll sling some trousers on before we go. Have I got time for breakfast?'

'Yes—go and change now while I make it. There's some bacon——'

'Bacon sandwich would be fantastic—thanks, Clare.'

He bounded up the stairs, and Clare's heart sank. He was so fit and vital, so much like Michael had been this time last week. How cruel of fate to send him now to taunt them. Perhaps he would be less insensitive with Michael than he was with her?

He was back in seconds, much less disturbing in a pair of light cotton trousers. 'How's that?'

'Better,' she said quietly. 'Thanks, Andrew. Here's your breakfast.'

They ate in silence, mainly because Clare made it obvious she didn't want to indulge in small talk, and then they left for the hospital.

'There's the car,' she told Andrew, pointing across to the doctors' car park. 'You can be independent now—have you got keys?'

He tossed them in the air and caught them with a flourish. 'Found them on the dresser. Right, let's get this over with.'

Clare gave him a keen look, and noticed the lines of strain around his eyes. 'I'm sorry—this must be hard for you, too—I'm so bound up with Michael's feelings I haven't really taken in anybody else's. Come on— I'm sure he'll be glad to see you.'

She took him up to the ward and left him in the day-room while she joined the others in Sister's office for the report.

Danny was quieter, much to everyone's surprise, and Pete Sawyer had had a better night. Barry Warner was still very depressed, but had slept better.

'In fact,' Judith Price said with relief, 'everyone seems to have had a better night, although Mr

Barrington was a little restless once or twice—probably
because he's not on pain relief any more.'

'None?' Clare said in surprise.

Judith Price shruggd. 'He refused it—I imagine he
knows his own limits. He said phantom limb pain was
just exactly that, and he wasn't afraid of ghosts! Right,
everyone, I'm off. See you tomorrow!'

Clare hung back until the others had left, and asked
Mary O'Brien if Michael's brother could visit him.

'Of course—how marvellous that he's here. I think
he's needed visitors—although Ross Hamilton's been
over a couple of times and his grandfather yesterday,
but still—yes, Clare, take him in. It's the best time,
really, as he's so busy with Physio now.'

So Clare went and found Andrew deep in conversation with Tim Mayhew, and took him down to
Michael's room. His likeness to Michael attracted quite
a lot of comment, but he was obviously used to it.

'He's in here,' Clare said, popping her head round
the door. 'Hi, there.'

Michael was standing by the window staring out. He
was dressed in boxer shorts and a short-sleeved shirt,
and was leaning on his crutches. He turned to her with
a serious look.

'Clare, about last night, we need to talk——'

She smiled. 'Not now. You've got a visitor.'

Andrew opened the door and walked in, then stood
looking at his brother for a long moment before he
spoke. When he did, his voice was husky.

'I didn't really believe it. . .'

Michael laughed, a hollow, sad laugh. 'Believe it,
Andy. It's true.'

'Oh, God, Mike——'

Before Michael could move Andrew was across the

room, enfolding him in a bear-hug. Clare heard a
broken sob, she wasn't sure who from. It probably
didn't matter. Turning quietly, she left them to it and
carried on with her work.

Tim Mayhew went in some half-hour later, and
stayed for a few minutes while Andrew lurked
uncomfortably in the corridor. His eyes were red-
rimmed and he seemed shaken.

Clare shot him an understanding smile. 'You don't
look as if you like hospitals.'

'Hate them. Never have been able to understand
how Michael could spend his life in them.'

She laughed. 'I think some of the patients would
agree with you.'

Tim came out and Andrew went back in for a short
time before taking himself off 'for a look round the
local metropolis' as he put it.

Clare had intended to take her coffee in to Michael's
room and drink it there, but he was down in Physio
and stayed there until nearly lunchtime, then after
lunch which he ate with Barry Warner he had a rest
before going back to Physio again for another hour.

She went off duty at four and he still wasn't back,
but she rang in the evening and was told that his
brother was with him.

She didn't go back in, but did some washing instead
and fidgeted restlessly with the house. In the end she
rang her mother and poured out all her worries, telling
her how he seemed to be avoiding her as far as it was
possible in the hectic atmosphere of the ward.

'I expect it's just reaction, dear,' she said vaguely.

'Probably,' Clare agreed, but she was getting more
and more worried.

She was in bed by the time Andrew came back, and

was gone before she saw him in the morning. Once
again Michael was avoiding her, but this time by
seeking company. He was getting competent on his
crutches, and as he swung past the entrance to Borstal,
Danny Drew called him over.

Clare was in the corner doing Pete Sawyer's pressure
areas, and she watched as Michael manoeuvred himself
over to Danny's bed and eased himself down on the
edge.

'The other day,' Danny said quietly, 'I was out of
line. I'm sorry, Doc.'

Michael nodded. 'That's OK, Danny. I understand.
How about a game of cards?'

'Pete's got some—here, Pete, borrow your cards,
mate?'

'Sure—here, Staff, could you give them to him?'

'Of course.'

Clare took the cards and walked over to Michael.
'Are you going to play patience?'

'Happy families, I thought,' he said with wry
humour.

They were still there half an hour later when Tim
Mayhew came on to the ward. By this time the card
game had deteriorated into a riot, with Michael showing the others card tricks and Danny outdoing him
right, left and centre.

'Good morning, Mr Barrington!'

Michael looked up at his boss and his mouth quirked
into a grin. 'Arr, Tim lad!' he said, brandishing his
crutches, and swung himself down the ward after his
despairing boss, leaving the young lads howling with
laughter.

'He's a great bloke, isn't he?' Danny said with a
touch of hero worship in his eyes.

'Yes, he is,' Clare agreed, her heart aching.

Mary O'Brien and Tim Mayhew echoed the sentiment a few minutes later.

'Doing really well,' Mr Mayhew said with satisfaction. 'His morale seems high, too.'

Privately Clare disagreed. Are they all blind, she thought miserably, or is it just because I love him that I can see he's dying inside?

'Mr Mayhew, is there any chance I could take him home for the weekend? I think he could do with anchoring himself in reality a bit. He doesn't really need nursing any more now, and I can do his stump dressing at home.'

Tim Mayhew gave her a keen look. 'You don't agree with me, do you?'

She shook her head. 'I think he's dreadfully depressed. I also think he's doing his best to hide it from everyone, because under the bonhomie he's such an intensely private person. I really think he needs to be at home for a while to come to terms with what's happened in privacy.'

He nodded slowly. 'You could be right. Well, so long as you watch him. When did you have in mind?'

'I'm off at twelve-thirty tomorrow until twelve-thirty on Sunday—that would give him twenty-four hours.'

Mr Mayhew nodded again. 'Sounds fine. OK, do that. I'll pop in and have a look at him tomorrow morning before you go, but I can't see any problems.'

There were none. At twelve-forty the following day Clare wheeled him down the corridor to the main entrance and over to her car. With a combination of stubborn pride, ingenuity and sheer brute strength he levered himself across the gap to the passenger seat and leant back, sweat beading his brow.

'OK?' she asked anxiously.

He shot her a weary grin. 'Fine. Take me home, Clare.'

They arrived at the cottage to find Andrew was nowhere to be seen. Clare climbed out of the car.

'Hang on,' she told Michael, 'I'll get Andrew to help.'

She walked into the kitchen and found him grinding coffee. She touched him on the arm to attract his attention.

Startled, he turned to her and covered his chest with his hand, laughing. 'God, woman, you scared me to death!' He turned off the coffee grinder. 'How is he?'

'OK, I think. Andrew, there's something I hadn't thought of—accommodation. Obviously I can't sleep with him in view of what's happened, but I must be here this weekend, I promised.'

'You could always sleep with me——'

'I don't think Michael would understand,' she said with a light laugh.

'No problem,' he said with a smile. 'I'll get my stuff out of your room now.'

'You do that,' Michael said from the doorway behind them.

Clare spun round and gasped at the white-lipped anger on his face.

'Michael, what's the matter?'

'I thought you'd grown out of that,' he continued coldly, looking over her head at Andrew with eyes like twin chips of ice, 'I was obviously wrong. You can do whatever you like in private—Clare and I are finished. Just have the decency not to do it in my home.' And with that he turned on his heel and stumbled out into the garden, slamming the door behind him.

CHAPTER SIX

AFTER a few seconds of stunned silence, Andrew strode out of the kitchen after his brother. Clare, shocked and appalled and totally confused, slumped against the table and listened in mounting horror to their raised voices.

'What kind of a bastard do you take me for?'

'If the cap fits—you've done it before, after all. Why not now?'

'Just thank your lucky stars you're in the state you're in, or I'd be tempted to knock some sense into you——'

'Yes,' Michael sneered, 'not even you'd hit a cripple, would you, you chicken-livered bloody hypocrite?'

'Don't push your luck!'

'Look, Andrew, just go away, would you? Even the sound of your voice makes me sick. And take Clare— I don't want to see her either.'

'Clare's done nothing—I've done nothing. Why the hell are you so steamed up? You're so bloody jealous you've lost your reason!'

'Get out of here.'

'Look, Michael, for God's sake——'

'I said *get out*!'

There was an endless stretch of silence, and then a car door slammed, the engine roared to life and with a great splutter of gravel Andrew tore off down the lane. Through the window Clare saw Michael's shoulders slump.

109

Taking a deep breath, she went out into the garden.
'Come and lie down and rest,' she said gently. He
shook his head.

'Leave me alone.'

'Michael, you need to lie down—you look awful.'

He turned towards her then, staring at her with eyes
that blazed with hatred.

'Whose fault is that?'

She ignored him, unable to answer because of the
dreadful pain inside.

'I'll find you a sun lounger—I think there's one in
the shed.'

She found it, and after a few seconds managed to
open it. She reached for his arm. 'Here, let me help
you.'

'I can manage.'

'Suit yourself.'

Desperately hurt and confused, Clare turned away.

'I'll get your room ready,' she threw over her
shoulder, and went up into the bedroom she had shared
with him before the accident, sat on the edge of the
bed and cried.

When the tears finally slowed to a halt, she gathered
her things together and moved them into the spare
room, repacking Andrew's clothes and possessions that
were strewn carelessly across the room. She changed
both beds, turned Michael's down ready for him and
unpacked his wash-things in the bathroom.

Finally there was nothing left to do, so she went
back downstairs and out into the garden. Michael was
asleep in the dappled shade of a willow tree, O'Malley
sprawled possessively across his chest. He mumbled
something in his sleep and shifted restlessly. O'Malley
stood up, stretched, kneaded his claws in Michael's

shoulder and with a lithe leap faded into the undergrowth.

Michael rubbed his shoulder and sat up. 'Damn cat,' he muttered, and then he noticed Clare.

'You're still here,' he said flatly. 'I thought you would have gone.'

She shook her head. 'Sorry. I'm not going anywhere until we've talked—or at least, until you've talked.' With a superhuman effort, she met his eyes. 'What did you mean when you told Andrew that we were finished?'

He looked away, his jaw working.

After a long time, he said, 'I think we were hasty. We thought we were in love, but we were in love with love—with a dream. It's just as well this happened when it did, Clare—it's given me time to think.'

'And you think I don't love you?'

'No,' he returned unevenly, 'I know that I don't love you. I'm ready to settle down, but—I misread the signals. Let's face it, Clare, you're a beautiful woman, and when a beautiful woman throws herself at your feet, it takes a hell of a man to walk away.'

She swallowed the hurt, aware of the truth behind his barbed comment, and hung her head.

'Even so,' he continued, 'it hurt to think you'd replaced me so fast—and so cruelly. I can't blame him—God knows I found you irresistible——' His voice cracked, but he went on regardless. 'Tell me, Clare, what was my brother like—was he good in bed?'

Her pain coalesced into a boiling rage that wouldn't be contained. How *could* he? How could he even *think* it?

'Fantastic,' she lied, 'better than you, anyway.'

She heard the hiss of his indrawn breath and realised

she'd gone too far. Raising her head, she saw the pain in his eyes as he turned away from her.

'It's not the first time I've heard that, and I doubt it'll be the last,' he said bitterly. 'I'd like a drink.'

'Perrier?'

'Gin and tonic.'

'No.'

'Yes, damn it!'

'A weak one,' she compromised, and fled to the kitchen.

It was an endless day. Michael was unapproachable, and, in truth, Clare didn't know how to begin to talk to him. She knew she shouldn't have taunted him about Andrew, especially as there wasn't a grain of truth in it, but it was too late now. The words were out, and, like feathers from a pillow, were almost impossible to get back.

She helped him to prepare for bed in a fulminating silence, and lay awake for hours listening to the small sounds from his room. Surely he couldn't mean it? He must love her—they had been so close, so happy. Surely he didn't? Perhaps it was just depression, or misunderstanding what he had overheard, but surely— oh, God, she thought, please let it not be true!

When she fell asleep, finally, it was with Lottie's ring clutched in her hand, and tears still wet on her cheeks.

In the early hours she awoke suddenly, her heart pounding in the silence. Throwing back the bedclothes, she crept out of bed and stood listening on the landing.

Michael groaned, then with a sobbing scream he yelled, 'Clare, get out! Get out!'

She ran into his room and shook him gently awake.

'Michael? Michael, it's all right—you're dreaming. It's OK. It's OK, darling, hush—hush. . .'

Carefully, avoiding his left leg, she eased herself into bed beside him and put her arms round him.

'Clare?' he whispered hoarsely.

'Shh. It's all right now. It's all over.'

He groaned and sagged against her. 'I had a nightmare,' he mumbled. 'We were in a railway carriage, and—oh, God. It was true!' he muttered raggedly. 'Oh, no, Clare, I——'

She held him close as his body shook with silent grief, and she rested her cheek against his face, her own tears mingling with his as they fell.

Finally he slept, waking only as the sun slanted over the bed and bathed the room in golden light.

He shifted on to one elbow and looked down at Clare almost in disbelief.

'What are you doing here?' he asked gruffly.

'You had a nightmare—I didn't want to leave you.'

His hand came up and touched her cheek. 'You've been crying.' His eyes wandered over her body, her nightdress pulled taut over her breasts. 'God, you're lovely—I want you.'

'Michael, don't you think——?'

'I don't want to think. I don't care if it isn't good for me—I want you. I'd have to be dead not to want you. Come here. . .'

And because she was starved of his touch, because she longed for the tenderness and passion, the gentleness and the closeness, she went to him, meeting him touch for touch, kiss for kiss, shattered by the sudden explosion of sensation as he took her roughly, his mouth ravaging, his body almost cruel in its demands.

She cried out beneath him, and felt his body shudder violently under her hands as he collapsed against her in a devastating climax.

For a few seconds he fought for breath, then he levered himself away from her and fell back against the pillows, gasping for breath. His face was white, his forehead beaded with sweat.

'Michael——?'

'I'm sorry,' he muttered, 'I had no right to do that to you. It's just—the thought of you with Andrew——'

He turned his head away, the muscles of his neck taut with strain.

She reached out to him, her heart aching. Surely he didn't think——

'Darling?'

'Leave me alone, Clare, please.'

'Michael, about Andrew——'

'No! I don't want to hear. Just leave me alone.'

'But, Michael——'

'Clare, for pity's sake, can't you understand? I want to be alone!' he cried savagely. 'What do you want from me? Dear God, leave me the shreds of my dignity—don't make me crawl away from you on my hands and knees! I want to be *alone*!'

'I'm sorry—oh, God, I'm sorry—Michael. . .'

The sight of his rigidly averted face shattered the last fragments of her control, and she ran back to her room, slamming the doors behind her.

Even so, the sound of his racking sobs filtered through the old timbers and penetrated her misery. She stood numbly in her room, her hand pressed over her mouth, listening to the man she loved more than anything else in the world, coming to terms with the tragedy that had overtaken him.

Forbidden to help, and yet unable to stand by and listen to it without going to him, she dressed hurriedly and went out into the garden, tugging furiously at the weeds with her bare hands until she had made them bleed.

Astonished, she stared blankly at them. They didn't seem to hurt—and yet, now she was conscious of them, perhaps they did hurt. It was just a much smaller hurt than the iron band around her heart that tightened with every passing second.

She wandered into the kitchen, and stumbled to a halt. Michael was propped against the worktop, dressed in his shorts and shirt, his hair gleaming wetly from the shower. He looked—superficially, at least—calm and in control.

'You should have called me—I would have helped you.'

'I didn't need you,' he told her bluntly. 'I put a bag on my dressing, but it's a bit damp. Could you change it for me? It's rather awkward to reach, or I'd do it.'

'No, I—that's fine, of course I'll do it. Sit down.'

'There's no hurry—I made you a coffee. It's by the—hell, Clare, what did you do to your hands?'

She stared at them, and rubbed them against her jeans, trying hard not to wince. 'I—nothing. I was weeding. Must have pulled up some bracken or something. I'll put some antiseptic on them.'

She busied herself at the sink, washing the cuts, and Michael stood beside her, watching. Finally he lifted her hands and turned them firmly but gently palm-up.

'They're cut to shreds—oh, Clare. Let me dress them.'

'No, you're. . .'

'I'm what?' He met her eyes. 'Crippled?'

Her eyes widened. 'Don't say that!'

'Why not? It's true. Not my hands, though. I'm still a doctor—nothing's happened to change that. And frankly, the sooner I get back to work, the better. Now get the first-aid kit out of the cupboard there and come and sit down.'

In fact only one or two of the cuts were deep, and Clare wallowed in the agony of Michael's touch. He was so gentle—so different from the wild, crazy man he had been just a few hours before. When he had finished he picked up her hands and turned them over, inspecting the backs, then without releasing her he looked up and met her eyes.

'I'm sorry. I've brought you so much pain. Once, I thought we could have had so much together. Forgive me.'

She held his brilliant blue gaze until it blurred, and her tears welled over and splashed on to their hands, then she closed her eyes and pulled her hands away.

'There's nothing to forgive,' she said quietly. 'It isn't your fault.'

'I used you this morning. That was despicable.'

She laughed, a short, high, rather frantic little laugh. 'I used you too—or didn't you notice? You were the pits, Michael, but I was with you every step of the way. Let me do your leg.'

He sat in grim, tight-lipped silence while she changed the dressing on his stump. It was healing well, she noticed absently, relieved to see that there were no obvious adverse effects of their lovemaking. 'I expect Tim Mayhew will take some of the stitches out tomorrow,' she said as steadily as she could manage. 'It'll feel better then.'

'It feels fine,' he said curtly. 'Thank you.'

'You're welcome,' she whispered. Standing up, she moved away from him, away from the heat of his skin and the faint scent of him that clung to her senses, out of reach so she no longer had to touch his body or be touched by it.

'I'll go and get ready,' she said quickly, and turned and ran for the stairs.

When she came down he was still sitting there, O'Malley draped round his neck, his hair dry now. She held out her injured hand, palm up. On the dressing lay Lottie's ring in its box.

'You'll want this back,' she said calmly. 'I expect one day you or Andrew will get married. I hope she has better luck than we've had.'

He took it with fingers that were less than steady, and opened it, staring at the ring. 'Of course, it could still be yours—if you married Andrew you could have it all—the perfect hero *and* the ring.' He looked up at her, his eyes taunting. 'Of course he's not a doctor, but he's filthy rich——'

She struck him with the full force of her hand. 'How dare you?' she whispered raggedly. 'Andrew is nothing to me—nothing! I meant it—I still mean it! I love you——'

'No. No, Clare, you don't love me, and anyway, it's academic, because I don't love you. We'd better go if you don't want to be late.'

'I'm not going anywhere until we've sorted this out.'

He caught her wrist and pulled her hard up against him. 'Listen to me—I don't intend to say it again. What we had is over. Yes, I still want your body—who wouldn't? You're beautiful, and you make love like a cross between an angel and a houri, but that isn't going to influence me again. I'll be out of hospital in a few more days, and when I come back here I want you to be gone. Do you understand?'

'But you can't cope alone!' she protested. 'How will

you shop, and cook, and get to Physio, and all the other things you need to be able to do? You have to get the DVLC to grant you a licence before you can drive again—how will you cope out here in total isolation?'

'Taxis,' he told her bluntly. 'Mobile shops, hospital car service, and so on. I still have the telephone, Clare. I can summon anything I need——'

'And what if you fall? Who will pick you up?'

'I will.'

'You're crazy.'

'No.' His hand on her wrist gentled. 'No, Clare, I'm not crazy, not yet. But I soon will be if I don't get some privacy. I know I can't really cope, but I have to try, or I'll go round the bend.'

She sank down in front of him and rested her hand on his knee.

'I accept that, and I'll do everything I can to keep out of your way, but please let me help you at first—at least until you've got your artificial leg and you're confident on it. They'll do the cast on Tuesday, and take all the measurements, and then you should have it within a week. Let me stay till then—please? I'll keep away from you, stay in my room, whatever—but let me help you find your feet—please, Michael? And then I'll move out, I promise.'

He met her eyes with a look of such burning intensity she thought he was staring into her soul, and then his lids closed and he nodded in defeat.

'OK. Thanks.'

She stood up abruptly. 'Don't thank me—I'm doing it entirely for selfish reasons. Are you ready?'

'Yes,' he sighed tiredly. 'Yes, I'm ready.'

'Then let's go.'

* * *

The journey back to the hospital marked the first phase in their truce. They were both quiet, but it was an accepting kind of silence, a still period that they both needed in order to come to terms with the changes that had taken place in their relationship.

Clare still took an active part in Michael's nursing, but as he healed and spent more and more time in Physiotherapy, so he needed less and less care. He began taking an interest in his patients again, and spent much of his free time with Barry Warner.

On Thursday Clare went into Sister's office to find him in consultation with Tim Mayhew over Barry Warner's X-rays. She noticed that Pete Sawyer's notes were also out, and raised an eyebrow at the consultant.

He winked, and turned his attention back to Michael.

'Yes, I think I can safely say that you did an excellent job on young Warner. There are definite signs of healing in that right tibia—look, see the callus beginning to form here, and here—excellent. And young Pete Sawyer's radius and ulna are showing tremendous improvement. Congratulations. Now, what about you?'

'Can I go home tomorrow?'

Clare gasped, and Michael turned round and looked questioningly at her.

'I—I was going to arrange some time off, so I could be there——'

'That isn't necessary. I'll be fine. You're around enough—when are you off?'

She checked the rota on the wall. 'Sunday lunchtime to Tuesday morning—then I've got next weekend off completely. Can't you wait till the weekend?' she pleaded.

He sighed. 'Frankly—no, I can't. Clare, really, I'll

be perfectly all right. If you could bring me in on
Tuesday morning for my leg, then I can spend the day
in Physio practising, and go home with you at
four——'

'And then you'll be back at home all on your own
until Friday night, and I know you, Michael—you'll try
all sorts of things you aren't ready for, and fall over
and hurt yourself——'

'Clare,' Tim Mayhew interrupted, laying his hand
gently on her arm. 'My dear, he'll be quite all right.
He's a sensible man, and he knows his limitations. The
last thing he's going to do is end up back in here with a
fractured femur, isn't it?'

He swivelled round and glared at Michael, who gave
a wry chuckle.

'Yes, sir!'

'Right. So tomorrow it is. How will you get home?'

'I'm on a late—I'll pick you up in the morning,'
Clare said heavily.

'Right. I'll sort out the discharge papers, Michael.
Now, my dear, I wonder if you could come with me
and we'll have a look at Danny Drew. How do you
think he's doing?'

Clare allowed herself to be wheeled off to Danny's
bedside, and gave Mr Mayhew her assessment of
Danny's progress.

'Good, good—well, Danny, the physiotherapist
seems to think you're ready for some partial weight-
bearing exercise, and the X-rays we did yesterday back
that up, so we're going to get you down to Physio every
day now to get you walking again. Mrs Matthews will
explain all the exercises to you, and get you up and
about again as soon as we can. All right?'

Danny grinned, relief all over his face. 'Great, sir—

thanks. I can't tell you how good it'll be to be up again. Oh, sir—how's Mr Barrington?'

Tim Mayhew regarded him steadily for a second, and then squeezed his shoulder. 'He's going to be fine, Danny—just fine.'

'Wicked thing to happen,' Danny said quietly. 'He's a brave man. Will he be able to work again?'

'Oh, yes. Give him a few weeks to recuperate, and he'll be back, don't worry. I can't afford to lose him!'

Danny looked at Clare. 'Been tough on you, Staff, seeing as how you're going with him and so on.'

She summoned a smile. 'Oh, Danny, we're just good friends.'

'But you were very upset——'

'Of course I was. I—care about him. We all do. He's a valuable member of the team——'

Danny snorted, Tim raised an eyebrow and Clare sighed.

'Butt out, Danny,' Pete Sawyer called from the other side of the ward. 'None of your damn business what any of them feel.'

Clare was getting more flustered by the second.

'Really, we're just——'

'—good friends, I know. I'm sorry.'

Clare was astonished at the new maturity she saw in Danny's eyes—maturity, and understanding.

'Thank you,' she said quietly, and walked away, leaving Tim Mayhew to follow her.

'He's grown up,' Tim said as he caught up with her.

'Not before time,' Clare responded, wishing they could all leave her alone to wonder how she would cope with Michael at home on his own all day.

'He *will* be all right,' he said.

'What?'

'Michael. He'll be all right.'

Clare met his eyes, hers twin pools of misery and confusion. 'I hope so.'

'Oh, my dear. I was so afraid this would happen.'

Clare looked away. 'I'll cope. Perhaps with time. . . I must get on. Is there anyone else you want to see?'

There wasn't, so he left her to bury herself in ward routine to the exclusion of her troublesome thoughts.

That evening she went to the supermarket and stocked up on things he could graze on easily while she was out, and also made up a day-bed in the sitting-room near the french windows so he could rest if he needed to.

He was ready for her when she arrived at nine—more ready, at least, than she was, which wasn't difficult. He spurned the wheelchair, preferring instead to walk with his crutches. He was very proficient, but glared at his suitcase with undisguised loathing.

'I should be carrying that,' he grumbled.

'Oh, shut up. Why do you have to be Superman?'

He grinned at her. 'Now there's an idea. If I could fly everywhere——'

Clare laughed. 'Come on, cowboy. Let's get you home.'

The patients all called greetings to him, and Clare saw that he was touched by their good wishes. 'Just hedging their bets in case they're still in when I get back to work,' he joked, but she could see he was moved.

Mary O'Brien walked them to the door. 'See you soon, Michael,' she said gruffly, and to everyone's surprise, she hugged him. 'Mind how you go, now—you're not Superman!'

Which of course made his lips twitch into a smile.

'Did I say something funny?' she asked.

Michael shook his head. 'No. Clare just told me the same thing. I will be careful. Thank you for everything, Mary, you've been wonderful. If you ever decide to retire and open a guest house, let me know. I'll become a permanent resident.'

He looked at Clare.

'OK?' she asked him.

He nodded. 'Yes. Time to start living again.'

CHAPTER SEVEN

CLARE was on a late on Friday followed by an early on Saturday—which, in essence, meant that she saw precious little of Michael in the first twenty-four hours that he was home.

At first he was just simply tired, and relieved to be away from the busy hospital routine which had been his life for two weeks. He slept most of the time on the day-bed in the sitting-room or on a sun lounger under a tree in the garden, and didn't seem inclined to chat when he was awake.

When she helped him up to bed on the first night, he told her in no uncertain terms that he was getting used to the nightmares and, in the event of him having one, her presence would not be necessary.

Consequently, when she heard him cry out, she lay rigidly in her bed until she heard him moving about some time later. Then she opened the door a crack and watched as he shuffled down the stairs on his bottom to the kitchen, hopped over to the fridge with the aid of one crutch and got himself a drink. She closed the door softly before he turned round, and listened until she was satisfied that he was safely back in bed before allowing sleep to reclaim her.

Finally Saturday afternoon came, and she was able to spend the evening preparing a meal for them. He was watching television and ate his meal on his lap, barely speaking. He yawned several times, and seemed quite happy when she suggested that he might like an early night.

It was still only a quarter to ten, so she stayed downstairs after he was safely settled and watched a weepy film with a sad ending that left her feeling ragged. On her way to bed she noticed that Michael's light was still on, so she tapped and stuck her head round the door.

'OK?' she asked softly.

Perhaps it was the gentle lamplight, or the sadness of the film, but he looked suddenly terribly vulnerable lying there propped up on the pillows, a book in his hand, his face grave.

'Come here,' he murmured.

She went in cautiously, and perched on the end of the bed.

'I just wondered if you were all right. You seem very tired—you will tell me if you feel ill, won't you?'

'Of course I will—I know the risks.' He sighed. 'Thank you for everything you're doing for me. I realise it isn't easy, under the circumstances, and I know I'm not the world's best patient, but I am grateful, Clare.'

'Oh, Michael, you know you're welcome. You don't have to thank me.'

'Yes, I do. Anyone else would have just gone.'

Like Andrew, she thought. He'd rung the hospital once or twice, and had brought Pop in to see Michael, but had left him at the door and hadn't set foot on the ward or spoken to his brother since the row the previous weekend. Clare hadn't seen him since he'd been back to collect his things, but she gathered from Pop that he was in London for a few days before returning to Germany.

'Would you like me to take you to see Pop tomorrow afternoon?' she asked him now.

He gave her a rueful grin. 'He's mad with me at the moment. I don't think I can stand another telling-off. I tell you what I would love to do.'

'What?'

He studied his hands in silence for a second. 'Go windsurfing.'

Clare swallowed. 'Don't you have to wait for your beach activity leg before you can do that?'

He snorted. 'Be realistic. It'll never be the same again.'

'No,' she retorted, 'you'll only have to tolerate one freezing cold foot! That can only be an advantage!'

She couldn't believe she'd said it. As she sat waiting for a hole to appear and swallow her, there was a choked sound from the other end of the bed. Startled, she looked up to find Michael chuckling. As she watched, a smile crept up his face until he was laughing, his head thrown back, tears running down his cheeks.

She laughed with him, overwhelmed with relief to hear the joyful sound. Finally he stopped laughing and shook his head ruefully.

'Oh, Clare,' he said weakly, wiping the tears from his eyes, his body still shaken by the occasional chuckle. 'You're good for me, d'you know that?'

Their eyes met and held, and the laughter faded. His face sobered, and his eyes became suddenly sad. 'I'll miss you when you go,' he told her quietly.

She stood up, torn between running away and throwing herself into his arms.

She turned towards the door. 'No, you won't. You'll probably throw me out in the end.'

'Probably,' he agreed, 'but I'll still miss you.'

'I don't have to go,' she said, without much hope.

'Yes, you do.' He gave a gusty sigh. 'Goodnight, Clare.'

'Goodnight. Call me if you need me.'

He muttered something that she didn't catch, and clicked off the light. She pulled the door to and went to bed, her heart still very much with him all alone in the big brass bed.

He had the nightmare again that night, and every night that followed, but she let him get on with it and he never mentioned it. Sometimes he got up, sometimes he just seemed to go back to sleep again, and gradually, as they fell into their daily routine, she learned when to talk and when to leave him in peace.

On the Sunday she took him down to see *Henrietta*, and he sat in the car and stared broodingly out across the water, his expression fixed. In retrospect it seemed a bad idea, but at the time she had thought it might cheer him up.

He spent Monday at the hospital in the physiotherapy department, and on Tuesday she took him in early on her way to work.

It was the big day, the day when he would get his PTB, or patella tendon-bearing prosthesis—in a word, his freedom.

He came up to the ward with her and said hello to the staff and patients. Barry Warner, particularly, had missed his company and was delighted to see him. He was starting to make excellent progress, and would soon be having physiotherapy on his left arm now that the swelling from the dislocation had gone down. His right leg was off traction, and the soft tissue injuries had healed enough for his leg to lie in the bed beside the other, covered in a light dressing. He was to have skin grafting to give better cover in one or two areas, but otherwise was well on the way to recovery, albeit slowly.

Danny was up and about on crutches, his good spirits high as usual, but he was putting his cheer to good use and entertaining the elderly patients at the other end of the ward.

Pete Sawyer had been discharged, his patella and pelvis healed and his right forearm, still immobilised in plaster, now showing signs of union.

The other patient who was now with them after two weeks in ITU with an intractable pneumonia was Alan Beedale, the patient whose foot Michael had amputated in the train. In a twist of irony he was in Michael's old room, and Clare watched their encounter with interest.

Michael tapped on the door, swung through it and perched on the end of the bed.

'Hi, there. How are you doing?'

Alan Beedale turned to him and his face creased in a puzzled frown.

'Don't I know you?'

Michael gave a wry grin. 'Yes. I operated on you in the train.'

'That's right—I asked about—wanted to thank you for getting me out, but they said you were off sick. Then I come up here and I hear all these rumours——'

Michael swung his left leg into the air. 'No rumours.'

Alan Beedale drew in a sharp breath and looked back at Michael.

'Hell—I don't know what to say.'

'You don't have to say anything—it wasn't your fault. The carriage collapsed long after you were out.'

'The old girl—what happened to her?'

Michael looked down at his hands. 'She died. I stayed with her.'

Alan nodded. 'That's what they said, but I didn't believe it. Said you stayed with her and the firemen told you to get out, then the whole bloody lot came down——'

Michael stood up and smiled.

'All water under the bridge now. I'm glad to see you're making progress. I must go—get the leg today.'

'Yeah—they're coming to cast mine, I think. Let me know how you get on.'

He nodded. 'Will do. Take care now, and do what the nurses tell you—they're lethal with the needle if you're disobedient!'

As he turned away with a little wave, Clare saw the depth of distress in his eyes. It was obviously all a little too close to home.

She walked to the door with him, her presence a silent support.

'Shall I meet you for lunch?' she asked.

He looked down at her, his face still strained. 'Don't know—we'll see how it goes, eh?'

'OK.' She tried to smile, but she was perversely disappointed and it was a dismal effort. 'Good luck—hope it fits all right.'

He raised one eyebrow and gave a short laugh. 'It'd better—I'm relying on it. Thanks for the lift.'

And he turned and swung away down the corridor on his crutches, his powerful muscles bunching as he propelled himself confidently along.

She watched him out of sight and went back into the ward to kill time until she heard from him again.

He appeared at three, in jeans and trainers, still with

his crutches but—unbelievably—almost walking normally.

'Hi!' he said with a grin. 'Any chance of a cup of tea?'

'Oh, I expect I could knock you one up—did you have lunch?' Clare asked.

He shook his head. 'Too busy. I don't suppose there's any toast?'

She smiled. 'Not unless I make it.'

'Pretty please?'

'You old sweet-talker, you!' she said, her voice a little roughened with emotion. It was wonderful to see him walking again, and she could tell at a glance that his confidence was restored, his natural masculine arrogance back in full measure. Damn it, he was almost swaggering!

'Come into the kitchen—you're cluttering up my ward,' she told him firmly.

While she filled the kettle and put two pieces of bread in the toaster, he propped himself up in the corner between the wall and the worktop, folded his arms and grinned.

'You look very pleased with yourself—how did it go?'

'Brilliant—it's harder than I thought, but not too bad. I'd panic without the crutches, but in a few days I probably won't need them so much.'

'How does it feel?'

'The leg? Or standing up like a person again?'

'Michael, you were always a person,' she told him gently.

'Mmm.' His face lost its cocky arrogance for a moment. 'I didn't always feel like it, Clare. There were times—never mind. As for the leg—it feels kind of weird. Not uncomfortable, but very odd. It's quite hard to point it in the right direction, but once I've got used to it I expect it'll be easier.'

She nodded. 'Well, the competitors in the Paralympics don't seem to have much trouble pointing theirs in the right direction!'

He laughed, a wry chuckle definitely at his own expense. 'Give me time, my love,' he said drily. 'I don't feel quite ready for it yet.'

Her heart leapt at the endearment, and she busied herself with buttering his toast while she gave her overactive imagination a severe talking-to. It was just a figure of speech—Andrew used it, too, so it was probably an expression common in their family. In any case, it meant nothing now. She put the toast in front of him and avoided his eye.

He attacked the toast ravenously, and she made him a pot of tea and poured two cups. It was her tea-break—in fact, she had only taken a few minutes for lunch as well on the off-chance that Michael might appear—and so she felt no guilty conscience about abandoning her duties.

As a result she was with him when Ross Hamilton popped his head round the door and grinned.

'Hi, there. I heard it was the big day. How goes it?' he asked.

'Hello, Ross! Fantastic—see, new leg!' Michael waggled his artificial leg in the air.

'There'll be no holding you now, then,' he said with a laugh. Then he turned to Clare. 'I have an invitation for you two. Lizzi says would you like to join us for a barbeque this weekend—Saturday would suit us best, but if you're working, Clare, we can make it another day.'

'No, Saturday would be fine, if Michael hasn't got

anything else in mind?' She glanced at him, uncertain
how he would respond to this invitation now they were
no longer engaged. Did Ross know? Somehow she
thought not. Perhaps she ought to find time to see Lizzi
in the canteen and fill her in before the weekend.

He shrugged. 'Sounds wonderful.'

'Good. Bring your swimming things, we'll spend the
day lying by the pool. Must go, I've got a list at four
and I need to see my patients. Come over when you're
ready on Saturday—eleven or so? See you then.'

'I must get on, too, I have to go back to Physio,'
Michael said, putting down his cup. 'Thanks for the tea
and toast. Can you give me a lift home?'

'Of course—what time?'

He shrugged. 'When you're ready—four-fifteen?'

'Fine. See you then.'

'I'll wait at the car,' he told her, and made his way
slowly but fairly confidently up the corridor, whistling
softly to himself.

If he had thought it would all be plain sailing, Clare
thought later in the week, he was having a severe
shock. He was in the garden, practising walking without crutches. He managed fine on the straight bits, but
the corners were tricky, especially turning in to the
left. Time after time he lost his balance and toppled
over on to the grass, swearing copiously.

Clare was glad she was out of earshot, because,
judging by the dedication he was bringing to it, his
language was colourful in the extreme!

At one point he hauled the leg off and hurled it into
the shrubbery, and she didn't know whether to laugh
or cry. In the end she just watched, and he staggered
up on to his crutches and retrieved it with difficulty,

restrapping it and completing the manoeuvre faultlessly this time.

She went out into the garden and congratulated him. 'You did it!' she said, smiling broadly.

'So I should bloody well hope—I've practised enough times! Damn fool leg—I'm going to get one of the American ones with the flexible foot. They have a more sophisticated mechanism——'

'Michael, you're doing very well. It's only been three days. You must be careful not to make your stump sore—you've been hammering up and down wearing a groove in the lawn for the last two hours. Now come and sit down and have a drink.'

He seemed quite happy to oblige. He was obviously hot and tired, and sank down on to the bench with a satisfied grunt.

'Here.' Clare handed him a tall glass of chilled white wine with a generous splash of soda, and he rolled the cold glass over his face. 'Ahh!' he sighed, and smiled contentedly. 'That's fantastic.'

'You're supposed to drink it!' she said with a laugh.

'All in good time,' he told her, pressing the glass to his chest. 'God, I'm hot—I must be so out of condition.'

She was mesmerised by the sight of his broad chest, the shirt hanging open to reveal the soft scatter of gold curls beaded with moisture. Her body yearned for the touch of his, the hard pressure of taut muscle against her softer flesh. Biting her lip, she dragged her eyes away and moved further along the bench.

'Sorry, are the pheromones getting to you? I must reek,' he apologised.

'You hardly reek,' she told him, suddenly conscious of the heady combination of aftershave and clean, healthy sweat. 'I was just giving you more room, as you're too hot.'

She glanced up and met his eyes, and knew her lie was seen and understood.

He looked away, a muscle in his jaw working as he stared out across the fields. Draining his glass at a gulp, he stood up and headed for the door.

'I'm going to have a shower, then I think I might lie down for a while,' he said, his voice sounding curiously strained.

She watched him go, her body taut with need, and then buried her face in her hands.

It couldn't go on, living here with him, loving him, wanting him, and being held at arm's length all the time. And he didn't really need her that much any more.

She sighed. Tomorrow they were at Ross and Lizzi's house for the day, but the next day she would start looking for a flat.

Swallowing her tears, she went into the kitchen to prepare their meal.

Saturday dawned bright and clear. Already by nine o'clock it was getting hotter, and the forecast was hot, dry and sunny. Clare swung her slender legs out of bed and pulled on a long T-shirt, then made her way quietly down to the kitchen.

Michael was sitting at the table, his foot propped up on another chair, reading a BMJ.

'Oh,' she said, flustered, 'I thought you were still asleep.'

He glanced up, flicked his eyes over her from head to toe and returned his attention to the magazine. 'No, I've been up for some time. The kettle's hot.'

'So's the weather,' she commented. 'It's going to be a scorcher. Lovely for lounging by the pool.'

'Hmm.'

She shot him a glance. 'What's the matter?'

He looked up. 'Why should anything be the matter?'

'You don't sound very keen.'

He sighed and put down the magazine. 'I'm not. I don't know if anyone else will be there—Ross's sons, or other friends. . .' He shrugged. 'I'm not sure I'm ready for socialising yet.'

Clare lifted the receiver on the wall phone and punched in a number.

'What are you doing?' he asked sharply.

'Finding out—hello, Lizzi, it's Clare. I just wondered if there was anything you wanted us to bring with us— a salad, some wine, anything like that. I didn't know how many you were going to be catering for.'

'Just the four of us, the boys are with their mother, and no, don't bring anything except Michael—how is he, by the way?'

'Oh, getting to grips with his leg. The air was blue yesterday, but he's trying to run before he can walk at the moment. He'll be fine once he's got it sussed. Are you sure you don't want me to make a rice salad or anything?'

'No, really—just come when you're ready.'

'Lovely. We'll see you soon. Bye.'

She replaced the receiver and turned to Michael.

'Just us. You can relax.'

He snorted, then sighed. 'OK. I give in. I'll go and shower and get ready—it takes bloody hours.'

They left shortly before eleven, and all the way Clare was conscious of the tension in him. Despite the heat of the day, he was wearing jeans to cover his leg, although at home he had been happy in shorts. She wondered how difficult he would find taking off his leg and undressing to go in the pool with Lizzi around, but she knew there was nothing she could do to protect him from reality. He would have to find his own way of dealing with it.

Ross greeted them at the car and walked with them round the side of the house to the pool. Lizzi was lying in the shade of a tree, reading a book, and looked up as they approached.

'Hi, there. Drag up a chair—sun or shade?'

They all opted for the shade, and Ross brought them tall, clinking glasses of fruit juice from the kitchen.

Even so, the heat got to them. Ross lit the barbeque with a bit of help and advice from Michael in the way of good-natured abuse, and then they returned to the shade to flop on the cool grass.

Conversation was minimal but comfortable, Clare and Lizzi talking about the book she was reading, and Ross and Michael—of course—talking shop. After half an hour Ross stood up and flapped his T-shirt. 'Time for a swim,' he said, and with swift economy of movement he stripped off his T-shirt and shorts to reveal sleek black trunks.

'Michael, you coming in while the girls knock up some salad?' he asked, and Lizzi and Clare took the hint and made their way to the kitchen.

'I wondered how he would cope with that,' Clare said. 'I might have known Ross would work round it tactfully.'

'Does it trouble him much?' Lizzi asked.

'I don't know—he doesn't really talk about it all that much. Lizzi, I've been meaning to tell you—we aren't engaged any more.'

'What?' Lizzi put down the lettuce she was shredding and turned to Clare, her face touched with compassion. 'Oh, Clare, I am sorry. What happened?'

Clare sighed. 'I wish I knew. It was about a week after the accident, but he'd been getting more and more distant ever since the accident happened. I thought at first he was just depressed, but then I realised he just didn't want me around so much. Then he overheard me talking to his brother, and——' She lifted her shoulders in a defeated little shrug.

'Explain,' Lizzi said firmly, leading her to the table and sitting her down.

So she sat, and poured out all the happenings of the past three weeks, and Lizzi listened, her violet eyes troubled.

'So that's it,' Clare concluded. 'He doesn't love me, and as soon as he doesn't need me any more, I'll be moving out.'

'There's a flat coming up in the hospital,' Lizzi told her. 'My staff nurse, Lucy Hallett, is moving in with Mitch Baker, Ross's registrar, at the end of next week when Mitch gets his flat. They're both in hospital accommodation at the moment, but I know Lucy's got a nice little flat—would you like me to ask her what's happening to it?'

'Could you? I know the flat—it was near mine.' She sighed. She had only been out of the flat a month. Why had they been so hasty? Perhaps Michael was right after all.

They heard footsteps, and Ross appeared, his body glistening with water.

'Nice swim?' Lizzi asked him, accepting his damp kiss with a grimace.

'Fabulous,' he grinned. 'I've come for the chicken pieces and the kebabs.'

'In the fridge—where's Michael?'

'Still in the pool—he's trying to swim eight hundred metres.'

'He'll kill himself,' Clare said with a sigh.

'No, he won't,' Ross assured her. 'He's as fit as a flea—he's just a little out of condition at the moment, and hell bent on proving things to himself. He'll be fine. Is this all?'

He brandished the dish of kebabs and chicken pieces under Lizzi's nose.

'Oh, Ross, don't,' she said, turning away with her hand on her throat. 'Yes, it is all. We'll bring the salad down—is it OK for us to appear yet?'

'Oh, I think so. He's relaxed now, and having fun. If we ignore him he'll be all right.'

She tutted. 'I was hardly going to stare at him!'

'Sorry, darling.' Ross grinned, a lop-sided, little-boy grin, and hugged Lizzi with his free hand.

'Yuck, you're all wet. Go away!' she told him laughingly, and, picking up the salad dish, she followed him out. 'Clare, can you manage that tray?' she called over her shoulder.

Clare could. She followed them out, envying their camaraderie and obvious affection. As she walked down the steps behind them, she could see Michael powering up and down the pool in a swift, no-nonsense crawl that ate up the water.

Lizzi watched him for a second, and smiled. 'He's getting plenty of practice at tumble-turns, anyway.'

Clare nodded, and allowed her eyes to feast on the sight of his smooth, well-muscled arms cleaving through the clear water. Ross and Lizzi were dealing with the food, bantering good-naturedly about the readiness of the charcoal and the cooking time of the chicken pieces, and were quite oblivious to her presence.

Ross appeared at her elbow after a couple of minutes. 'Do you want to go in?'

She shook her head. 'No, not just yet. Perhaps later.'

'I just wondered. You were staring at the water with such longing.'

Lizzi took his arm. 'I don't think it was the water she was staring at,' she told him as she towed him away.

Clare closed her eyes. Was she so transparent? With a heavy sigh, she went into the shade and sat down, but it was still bakingly hot.

Lizzi came over and flopped on to the sun lounger. 'Why don't you take some of those things off?' she asked. 'You look steamed.'

'Good idea. I've got my costume on underneath. Perhaps when Michael's finished his marathon I'll go in and cool off.'

She peeled off her T-shirt and shorts, and kicked off her canvas shoes, wriggling her toes in the cool grass.

'That's better,' Ross said with obvious admiration.

'Hey, that's enough of that, you're spoken for!' Lizzi said laughingly.

He grinned. 'I can look, can't I? Artistic appreciation.'

She snorted. Clare bit her lip, and Lizzi tutted. 'Now you've embarrassed her. Go and cool off in the water.'

He laughed. 'It was only appreciation, not outright lust! She's a little too lush for me, I prefer my women rather more on the skinny side,' he said, leeering at his slender wife.

Lizzi hit him. 'I'll give you skinny, and less of the

plural, please! Women, indeed—you are too old for that sort of thing!'

He smiled tenderly and patted her tummy. 'I'm evidently not,' he said with undisguised pride.

Lizzi flushed and shooed him off. 'Go and turn the kebabs.'

'Nag, nag, nag,' he grumbled, but went anyway.

Clare looked across at her friend. 'Lizzi?'

She smiled with deep contentment. 'I'm pregnant—the baby's due in February.'

Emotion welled in her chest, and Clare reached out a hand blindly and grasped Lizzi's. 'Oh, Lizzi, that's fantastic! I'm so happy for you. . .'

She shut her eyes and tears welled over, splashing on to her bare legs.

'Oh, Clare, don't cry—I'm sorry, that was supremely tactless of us when you and Michael——'

'Clare and Michael what?' said Ross, coming back.

'Nothing, Ross. This is private.'

'No, tell him.' Clare struggled to her feet. 'I think I'll go for a stroll and have a look round your garden for a minute.'

She walked away, her head bowed, giving up the effort of keeping her tears under control. Maybe it would be easier to leave the hospital altogether, get right away from him once he didn't need her any more.

She found a bench tucked in under a tree at the far end of the garden, and sat down, indifferent to the beauty of her surroundings, all her attention focused on the yawning void of the rest of her life, a life that would be empty and meaningless without Michael.

A shadow fell on the grass in front of her, and she looked up to find him standing there, leaning on his crutches. He was still wet from the pool, the water making little rivers over his sleek skin.

'Lunch is ready,' he told her. He sounded concerned.

'I'm not really hungry.'

'Neither am I,' he confessed, 'but they've gone to a lot of trouble, and I think we should eat it. Come on, love. We don't have to stay too long.'

But it's not them I don't want to be with, she longed to tell him, it's you, because every time I look at you my heart breaks a little more——

'I'm coming.' She stood up and waited while he turned round, and walked slowly back with him across the gently sloping grass to the pool.

Despite her reservations she ate well, and so did Michael, and then after lunch they lay around for a while in the shade. Michael dozed, his arm flung up over his eyes, and then when he woke up they all went in the pool and played a rather wild game of individual water polo, with broken rules abounding.

Once the ball came towards Clare and she seized it, only to find herself being tackled enthusiastically by Michael, his body hard and sinuous against hers as he laughingly reached round her and grabbed the ball. After that she lost her concentration and ended up with the lowest score.

They left late in the day, after what had turned into a very enjoyable and relaxing afternoon.

'They're lovely people,' Michael said on the way home. 'They said if I could get over there, I could use the pool any time I wanted.'

'I can bring you over,' Clare found herself offering. He didn't comment, but she noticed his hands clenched on the grip of his crutches. Was it her, or just that he hated to be dependent? She didn't know.

They had tuna and salad sandwiches for supper, and Michael went up to bed early, tired after his exertion in the pool. Clare tidied up the kitchen and was putting her uniform in the washing-machine when there was an almighty crash above her head.

Dropping everything, she ran up the stairs and into Michael's room. He was just picking himself up off the floor, and she caught the tail-end of a string of profanities. He straightened up, naked, and glared at her.

'Are you all right?'

'Of course I'm bloody well all right! Damn it, woman, stop hovering!'

'Don't shout at me!' she yelled. 'I can't help caring about you!'

Suddenly it was all too much. Dropping her face into her hands, she burst into tears.

'Oh, God, Clare, don't cry,' he pleaded gruffly. 'I'm sorry. Ah, love, come here——'

She somehow ended up in his arms, the steady beat of his heart under her ear, his back firm and warm beneath her hands. He pulled her down gently on to the bed and rocked her against his chest, murmuring soothingly as she cried out all her pain. Then he tipped her head back and stared down at her, his eyes dark with emotion.

'God forgive me, Clare,' he whispered raggedly. 'I've tried—lord knows I've tried, but I can't resist you. . .'

He made love to her then, tenderly at first, and then with rising passion to match her own, clinging to her at the end as if he would never let her go.

They slept tangled in each other's arms, waking in the night to make love again slowly in the darkness.

When she woke, it was with a feeling of contentment

and well-being that had been absent for weeks. She stretched and opened her eyes, to find Michael propped up on one elbow, studying her with a haunted expression in his eyes.

'Hi,' she murmured, and reached up to touch him. He caught her wrist and held it, lowering it slowly to the bed.

'No,' he said quietly. 'I didn't mean last night to happen. I'm not going to apologise, I had warned you, and I can't lie and say I regret it, because I don't, but we mustn't let it happen again.'

She closed her eyes and rolled away from him, numb with shock. She had thought last night changed everything, whereas, of course, it had changed nothing at all.

'I'll be moving out at the end of the week,' she told him, and was appalled to find her voice shook. 'Lizzi's staff nurse is vacating her flat in the residence—I'll see if I can get it.'

'I think it would be as well,' he said softly, and she was surprised to hear the tremor in his voice, too.

She slid out of the side of the bed and picked up her clothes from the floor, then walked out of his room, closing the door quietly behind her.

They avoided each other for the rest of the day. Lizzi rang to say that no one had taken Lucy's flat and, provided she checked with the accommodation officer, there wouldn't be a problem.

So that was that. Clare spent the afternoon in her room drafting a letter of resignation, which she handed in to the chief nursing officer the following morning. She wasn't surprised to be called in to see her later in the day.

'Why, Staff? You're one of our best nurses, and as far as we've been aware, you've been happy here.'

'It's personal,' Clare told her, twisting her hands together in her lap.

The CNO straightened the letter in front of her, and then looked up at Clare.

'There were a lot of rumours about you and Mr Barrington, both before and after his tragic accident.'

Clare looked away. 'It didn't work out.'

'For him.'

She nodded. 'Please, I really don't want to talk about it. . .'

'How about if we moved you to a different department—perhaps out to the cottage hospital? There's a vacancy there for a sister—you could apply for that.'

Clare shook her head. 'It's not far enough.'

The elderly woman behind the desk stood up and came round, laying her hand on Clare's shoulder.

'You'll never outrun your memories, Clare, no matter how far you go.'

She sighed. 'I know that, but maybe if I get right away I'll be able to forget him sooner—damn. . .'

A tear splashed on to her hand, and another one. The CNO handed her a box of tissues and quietly left the room. After a few minutes Clare pulled herself together and returned to the ward, to find Mary O'Brien waiting for her.

'I'm going to miss you,' she said briskly, 'but I think you're right. It won't do either of you any good to fall over each other all day long at work. Now, why don't you go home? I can manage without you for the rest of the day, and you look as if you could do with some time to yourself.'

Clare shook her head. 'No, Mary, let me stay, please? I haven't got anywhere to go except here.'

'Sure?'

'I'm sure.'

'Right, well, in that case you can give Deborah Lewis a hand with the post-ops that have come back from Recovery. There are two arthoscopies, and a hip replacement, and when she comes down there's a young woman with bunions who's had a bilateral metatarsal osteotomy.'

'Right. I'll get on. And Mary?'

The sister looked up.

'Thank you—for everything.'

She smiled understandingly. 'You're welcome.'

The day went quickly after that. Somehow, making the decision to leave and having it accepted made her feel more positive, although she was still dreading facing Michael again when she got home.

She needn't have worried. There was a note for her propped up on the kitchen table.

> Dear Clare, This isn't working. If you need to contact me, I'm on *Henrietta*. Please feed O'Malley and let me know when you move. Michael.

He was gone.

CHAPTER EIGHT

LUCY HALLETT moved out of her flat on Friday afternoon, and Clare moved in on Saturday. It took a
couple of trips in her little car—when she had moved
in with Michael, they had used his Volvo estate, which
had swallowed up all the boxes of bits and pieces and
memorabilia with ridiculous ease.

She was just standing in the kitchen indulging in a fit
of nostalgia when there was a roaring and a spurt of
gravel outside. Seconds later, Andrew strolled through
the door.

'Hi. How's it going?'

'I don't know about it, but I'm going—I've got a flat
and I'm moving out.'

He swore, softly but succinctly. 'He surely doesn't
still think we had an affair?'

Clare sighed and sat down heavily. 'Andrew, I don't
know what he thinks any more. He wouldn't let me
explain, wouldn't talk about it. All he would say is that
he doesn't love me.'

'So why are you still here?'

'Because he needed looking after by someone, and I
was the only one available.'

'Damn.' He dropped into another chair and leant on
the table, propping his chin in his hand. 'Clare, I'm
sorry. I should have been here, but I was so mad with
him—he's always had this thing about me taking his
women——'

'And do you?'

146

He had the grace to look uncomfortable. 'I have done in the past—mainly to prove I could do it, and I wasn't the only one. We were always pretty competitive with girls, and sometimes we'd swap just to see if they noticed. But there was one girl—I don't know, we just had the chemistry, I suppose, and she got on better with me than she had with him—they had a showdown, and she said some pretty hurtful things to him. That was the last time I did it, though, and there's no way I would have tried to come between you, with or without his accident. He needs someone like you, Clare. He's a loner by default, really. He doesn't like being alone, but not many people can put up with his temper.'

She laughed. She had certainly seen plenty of evidence of that in recent weeks. In fact, this week alone without him had seemed unbearably quiet.

'Will you do me a favour? He's living on *Henrietta* until I move out—would you go over and tell him I've gone, and bring him back?'

'Sure. Do you want me to do it today?'

She nodded. 'I think so. I worry about him down there on his own. And Andrew. . .'

'Yes?'

'Try and make it up with him. He was very upset after your row, and I know he's missed talking to you. Pop's mad with him too for some reason—he's going to need you, if you can heal the breach.'

'I'd intended to try—that's why I'm here. I'll go over now.'

She stood up and gathered the last of her things. 'I've stocked the fridge and freezer up with food so he won't have to worry about that for a few more days, and I fed the cat this morning. The beds have both got clean sheets on, and I've hoovered everywhere——'

She broke off, and bit her lip.

'Do you want me to give him a message?'

'No. There's nothing to say, really, is there? You could give him my love, but there's not a lot of point. I'm off. Take care of him for me, Andrew.'

She reached up and kissed his cheek, and he hugged her gently.

O'Malley came in and wound round her ankles, and she bent and smoothed his fur. 'Bye bye, you old rascal,' she whispered unevenly, and then she left, without looking back.

She didn't see him again for almost two weeks, although she heard about him from Ross and Lizzi. Andrew had delayed his return to Germany for a few days and had patched up their quarrel, and while he was there he had taken Michael to Ross and Lizzi's to swim every day, and they had taken *Henrietta* out a few times.

Michael no longer came in to the physiotherapy department, and she discovered from Tim Mayhew that he was coming back to work on the Monday—five weeks and three days after the accident. He would be there for a week with Mr Mayhew, and then the consultant was off for a fortnight on holiday, and Michael would be on his own.

By all accounts he was fit and well, and adjusting rapidly to life without his leg.

Clare wished she were adjusting as fast. The days seemed endless, and the nights—the nights were the worst. Long, lonely nights, racked with dreams which left her aching for his arms.

She thought she would win a place in the *Guinness Book of World Records* for the number of tears shed in any given period. On the Thursday afternoon Deborah Lewis cornered her in the kitchen.

'You look awful,' she said bluntly. 'I'm going to a party tomorrow night, and I don't fancy going on my own. David's away, and I would appreciate some company, and I think it would do you good. How about it?'

'Oh, Deborah, I don't think I'd be very good company——'

'Come on! I won't take no for an answer. I'll meet you outside the residence at half-nine, OK?'

Clare sighed. 'Oh, OK, but I'm warning you, I'll be miserable.'

'Rubbish. What you need is a little cheering up. A bit of booze, a bit of male attention—lots of doctors there, all those sexy young housemen—you never know, you might meet someone.'

She laughed. 'Deborah, shut up. I've said I'll come, let's leave it at that.'

So there she was at the party with Deborah, fending off advances and wondering how quickly she could get away, when Michael came in, leaning on a stick, in the company of a stunning redhead.

She looked up and met his eyes, and her heart turned over. He looked tanned and healthy, but there was something missing—some vital spark that had disappeared at the time of the accident. He held her gaze for a few seconds, and then deliberately turned his attention back to the woman at his side.

Thereafter he ignored her. She didn't know how he did it—easily, probably, if he didn't love her—but there was no way she could ignore him. Her eyes followed his every move—and hers.

Deborah appeared at her side with a drink and shoved it into her nerveless hands.

'Have this—you look as if you need it.'

She sipped and grimaced. 'Who *is* that woman?'

'The redhead? Jo Harding, Obs and Gynae senior reg. Stunning, isn't she?'

Clare made a choked noise. 'I hate her,' she muttered.

'Look, love, it's going to happen,' Deborah told her matter-of-factly. 'He's a hell of a man, and let's face it, losing part of his leg isn't exactly going to affect his performance, is it?'

Clare flushed.

'Sorry, that was tactless. Do you want to go?'

She shook her head. 'No. I know it's stupid, but perhaps if I see him with her for long enough, I'll get to hate him.'

'That's the spirit—talking of which, get that brandy down your neck.'

She toyed with it for half a miserable hour, and then fed it to a plant. Michael and Jo Harding had disappeared and there was no sign of Deborah. She decided to go, and went upstairs to look for Deborah and tell her that she was going to make her way home. The stairs were cluttered with people chatting and laughing, escaping from the endless beat of the music in order to catch up on gossip and build bridges into new relationships. She squeezed between them, and found herself on the landing in a queue for the loo.

'Anyone seen Deborah Lewis?' she asked, and then a door opened behind her and Michael and Jo Harding came out of a darkened room together. His hair was rumpled, his shirt untucked, and he looked—she swallowed. He looked sexy as hell.

Jo smiled at him, her eyes warmly appreciative. 'Better?' she purred, her voice deep and husky.

'Wonderful—thank you, Jo.'

'Any time,' the redhead replied. 'I enjoyed getting my hands on that gorgeous body!'

He laughed, a slow, sexy laugh that Clare knew well, and turned towards the stairs.

There was no way to escape. His eyes met hers and his lips parted as if he was going to speak, but then he squeezed past her, his body hot and hard against her, and she could have wept. Then Jo passed her, her curves soft and lush on her tall frame, and Clare had to clench her fists so she didn't scratch her eyes out.

She gave them a few minutes to get out of the hall, then she made her way down the stairs and through the front door.

On the way out she met Ross and Lizzi coming in, and her distress was so apparent that Lizzi took her on one side and calmed her down, gradually extracting the story from her after a few incoherent minutes.

'The rat!' she said when Clare had finished. 'How could he? I mean, fair enough to have a relationship, perhaps, but to be so public—I really would have thought better of him.'

Ross offered to drive her home, and Lizzi quickly agreed.

'I didn't want to go to the party anyway, but it was someone in Ross's department so we thought we should—we'll blame it on the baby!'

Clare sat in the back of Ross's car as it purred quietly back to the hospital, totally unaware of her luxurious surroundings. When they pulled up, Ross and Lizzi got out of the car and Ross opened her door.

'Your destination, ma'am,' he said with mock deference.

She summoned up a smile and climbed out of the car. Her legs felt as if they would hardly hold her. She thanked them for the lift, and then out of habit she offered them a coffee.

'I'm afraid it's only instant, or you can have tea or fruit juice.'

'Clare?'

She turned towards them at Lizzi's softly voiced enquiry.

'Are you being polite, or would you like some company?'

She stared at her feet. 'Actually, all I really want to do is crawl into a corner and cry my eyes out,' she confessed miserably.

'Right.' Lizzi took Ross's arm. 'Come on, we're going home. Come over and see us if you want company any time. Don't sit inside your flat until you get cabin fever.'

Thanking them, she made her way back to her flat and let herself in, sagging back against the door. Damn it, she thought, how *dare* that bloody woman get her hands on him? 'He's mine!' she sobbed. 'Mine! You can't have him!'

She already has, a little voice taunted, and Clare picked up a nearby vase and hurled it against the wall, before crumpling against the door and letting the tears fall yet again.

On Sunday she went for a drive, and found herself out near Michael's cottage. Parking near the end of the track which led to it, but out of sight, she walked towards the cottage, ready to duck behind the hedge if he appeared.

As she reached the entrance into the drive she saw Ross's car parked beside the Volvo, and her steps faltered. Then she heard footsteps on the gravel, and quickly hid behind a shrub.

As they approached, she heard Ross speaking.

'I think you're being a fool. You obviously love her—why not give her the benefit of the doubt?'

'Oh, Ross, I can't risk it. She can't love me—not after such a short time. If I'd met her after the accident, I would be more sure, but it was so sudden, so quick. One minute I didn't know her, and the next we were engaged. We didn't have any time to get to know each other, but I know her better now, and I know she'd stand by me even if she hated my guts. She's that kind of girl, Ross. She takes commitment seriously. That's why I can't hold her to it. I had to let her go.'

'Maybe she doesn't want to go? I think she loves you, Michael—genuinely, truly loves you. I think you're doing her a grave injustice by not believing her.'

Michael laughed, a harsh, bitter laugh. 'Oh, no. You should have heard her in the train, begging me not to take the other bloke's foot off because he would be a cripple. When I came round, all I could hear was her voice saying that, over and over again—he'll be a cripple, he'll be a cripple—God almighty, Ross, you have no idea what I went through. Losing my leg was nothing; waking up to the realisation that I'd lost Clare was infinitely worse.'

'But she's stood by you, Michael—has she ever said anything to make you think she finds your injury unacceptable, or pities you? Do you really think she finds you unattractive?'

There was a lengthy silence, during which Clare remembered all the times she had had to shove her hands in her pockets to keep from touching him. Unattractive? She almost laughed aloud.

'I don't know,' he said eventually. 'She's too sensitive to my feelings to be that transparent. She pretends all this empathy, but I know it's just pity, really.'

'I don't think so,' Ross replied. 'I think she loves you, and your leg doesn't matter a damn to her. Of course she's sorry it happened—we all were. You can't hold that against her. Good grief, man, she'd be a callous bitch if she felt nothing! Can I give you my honest opinion? I think you're wallowing in self-pity, and I think you're afraid. I think you're crippling yourself, emotionally, to punish yourself for staying in that carriage when she wanted you to get out. I think you're trying to turn yourself into a hero to make up for what you perceive as your inadequacy—and I think you're a fool, because you're throwing away the love of a good woman for the sake of your pride.'

'That's rubbish!'

'Is it? Think about it. Come on, Lizzi will be waiting.'

She heard the car doors slam, and ducked lower behind the hedge as the car reversed out of the drive and then pulled slowly away down the track. Peering carefully through the leaves, she could see Michael sitting in the front of the car next to Ross, staring rigidly ahead.

She watched the car out of sight, then straightened her aching legs and stood up. O'Malley came running up, and she absently lifted him and draped him round her neck. He purred furiously, overjoyed to see her again.

'Tell me something, O'Malley,' she said shakily. 'If

he loves me, then why is he sleeping so openly with that damned redhead?'

O'Malley squawked and rubbed his head against her cheek.

'That's just what I think—she's a brazen tart. Damn it, she's only known him a few weeks!' she exclaimed in disgust, and then rather belatedly remembered her own speedy fall from chastity in his arms. 'I wonder if he gives her the same old line about being her other half?' she asked the cat in a choked voice.

Disentangling him from her hair, she set him down and walked back to her car, her thoughts confused.

If he did love her, as Ross suggested, and if he was so heartbroken at ending their relationship, then that could explain how he had found it so difficult to live with her, and why he had allowed himself to weaken and make love to her on the two bitter-sweet occasions that his rigid self-control had lapsed—but if that was the case, as she would dearly love to believe, then why that damned redhead?

'Joanna Harding, I hate you!' she muttered.

She started her car and crashed the gears, finally managing to locate reverse and turn it round before heading back to the hospital.

Tomorrow he was back at work. Tomorrow she would see him again. Tomorrow, maybe, she would get some answers.

Tomorrow.

God, how she dreaded tomorrow!

On Monday morning, Michael appeared on the ward at eight, just as Clare finished taking the report from Judith Price. He was walking with a stick, but she sensed it was for moral support as much as anything, as his gait seemed almost perfectly normal.

'Good morning, Staff,' he said in a civil but slightly distant voice.

'Good morning,' she replied stiffly, wondering how on earth she was going to get through the next few minutes, never mind the weeks until she left. 'It's good to have you back.'

He met her eyes for the first time, and smiled slightly. 'It's good to be back. Perhaps you could take me round and fill me in?'

'Certainly. Where would you like to start?'

He glanced at his watch. She noticed that it hung loosely on his wrist, as if he had lost weight. 'I think I've got time to see them all, but perhaps I'd better see the pre-ops first to have a chat.'

'Fine.' She led him to the second bay, opposite the nursing station, where the pre-operative patients were being prepared for Theatre.

'This is Mrs Green, who's having an arthroscopy to investigate a possible meniscal tear.'

'Yes, hello again. We met in Outpatients a few weeks ago. How's your knee been?'

He perched on the bed and chatted to her for a few minutes, explained again what they were going to do and marked the limb with an indelible pen.

'Don't want to get the wrong one!' he said with a grin, and moved on to the next patient.

He was calm, steady and efficient, moving from one patient to another without haste and yet without wasting any time on unnecessary chat, and without giving the impression that he was rationing their time. After the pre-ops, he examined the post-ops, and then went in to see Barry Warner, who was making heavy weather of his recovery.

'Michael—you're back in the saddle again! Good man. How's it going?'

Only then did she see the slightest flicker of emotion across his features, and it was so slight and gone so quickly that nobody else would have noticed.

'Fine,' he replied. 'How about you? How are the legs? I gather from the X-rays that you're progressing well.'

He examined Barry's legs gently, and then replaced the covers. 'Those skin grafts have taken well, Barry. I think we could start getting you up now on partial weight-bearing exercises. We don't want you forgetting how to walk,' he said with a grin.

As they left, he asked Clare how Danny Drew had got on.

'Oh, he made good progress. He went home a couple of weeks ago, still on crutches and coming back for physio. He pops in every now and again to see us and visit some of the inmates.'

'And Pete Sawyer?'

'You should see him in Outpatients. He's doing fine, I gather. His cast comes off this week.'

'Good. Let's hope he gets some mobility back in that hand soon. Right, I must go up to Theatre. Thank you, Staff.'

'My pleasure, sir,' she said drily to his departing back.

She went to check on the pre-ops and give them their pre-med. Mrs Green was first on the list.

'What a lovely man he is—I'm so glad it's him doing my knee. He's given me such confidence.'

Clare forced herself to smile. 'That's what it's all

about, Mrs Green. It'll soon be over and you'll be up and about again in no time.'

'Looked as if he'd been in the wars himself with that stick—what's he done, sprained his ankle playing squash or something?'

Clare's smile slipped.

'No, he lost his left leg below the knee in an accident five weeks ago. It's his first day back.'

'Oh, my lord! Well, the poor boy!'

Clare forced a laugh. 'Believe me, Mrs Green, the poor boy's fine. Now, let's just give you this injection to make you drowsy and dry up your mouth a little. Staff Nurse Lewis, could you check for me?'

Deborah joined her at the drug trolley, checked the Omnopon and scopolamine, and hissed, 'What happened to you on Friday? One minute you were there, and the next—pouf—you'd gone!'

Clare sighed. 'Not now. I'll tell you later.'

'Too right you will. Hello, Mrs Green. How are you?'

'Oh, all right, dear. Looking forward to having this over, actually.'

'Soon be done,' Deborah said cheerfully, and went on to the next patient. 'Hello, my love. How are you today?'

Not another one who uses 'my love', Clare thought in despair. 'Just a little pinprick,' she said mechanically, and injected the drugs with practised ease.

It was a good job her ease was practised, too, she thought later, because she was definitely functioning on auto-pilot.

Mary O'Brien came on at twelve-thirty, and Clare gratefully handed over and went for lunch.

Murphy's Law was obviously firing on all four cylinders, she thought bitterly as she sat down with her lunch. Michael, hair damp from the Theatre showers, was sitting diagonally across the room with his back to her, sharing a table with the *femme fatale* herself.

Clare stabbed a cherry tomato with her fork.

'Vicious!' said a voice behind her, and she looked up to find Ross balancing a tray with one hand. 'Mind if I join you?'

She shook her head. 'Of course not.'

He pulled up a chair and sat down beside her, then as he looked up, he saw Michael and Jo.

He swore softly.

'Quite,' Clare said with dry humour. 'They appear to be inseparable.'

'Yes. Clare, I'm sorry. I tried talking to him, but he wouldn't listen. Whatever he has going with Jo, I don't think it's serious.'

'Probably just recreational sex,' she said baldly, stabbing another tomato. 'I wouldn't be surprised—he has a high sex drive.' Ross choked. 'Sorry, that was unnecessary and personal. Please forget I said it.'

'Maybe I should. Are you OK? You sound very bitter.'

'I am, I suppose. Ross, do you think he really is trying to punish himself for the accident?'

Ross shot her a startled look. 'What gave you that idea?' he said quietly.

'I heard,' she told him. 'I went to see him yesterday—I don't know why, I don't know what I hoped to achieve. Some answers, maybe. Anyway, as I reached the cottage you came out on to the drive and I overheard you talking.'

'Where were you?'

'Behind the hedge.'

'And what did you hear?'

She sighed. 'Enough to confuse me. If he loves me, Ross, if he really was upset, then why is he having lunch with that bloody piranha?'

'He's only having lunch, Clare.'

'He wasn't on Friday!'

'No.' Ross cleared his plate, then pushed it away. 'I don't know what the answer is, Clare. Why don't you ask him?'

She shook her head emphatically. 'No. No, I couldn't, Ross. I've given him ample opportunity to climb down—I'm not going to grovel to him to take me back. If he wants to run around with that whore, then let him.'

'Hey, Clare, that's a bit much. Jo's a decent woman——'

'She doesn't look it!'

Ross smiled. 'Neither do you, but it doesn't stop you having a brain and a complex set of morals. Don't judge her by her appearance, Clare. She's all right.'

'She's also single, lonely, and on the look-out for a mate.'

Ross sighed. 'I can't argue, but I think you're jumping to conclusions, Clare.'

Just then Michael stood up, leant over the table and brushed Jo's lips with his before leaving.

'You really think so?' she said drily. 'That looked pretty conclusive to me. Do you want a coffee?'

'No, thanks.' Ross pushed back his chair and followed Michael out, his long stride easily closing the gap between them.

Clare sighed. She didn't really want the rest of her salad. She watched in despair as Jo Harding stood and walked over to the coffee jug. Tall, sinuous, she moved with an easy grace unusual in a woman of her height. As Clare watched, Jo turned towards her and met her eyes. She thought she saw sympathy there—sympathy, and something else that could have been envy.

God knows what Jo could see in her own. She was hesitating now, and Clare had an awful feeling that she was going to come over and talk to her. Unable to bear it, she shot back her chair and all but ran out of the canteen.

Michael came round the ward later that afternoon, and after seeing his patients came into the sister's office where Clare and Deborah Lewis were discussing the duty rota with Mary O'Brien.

'That's your last day, isn't it?' Deborah said, and Clare heard Michael's sharply indrawn breath.

'Clare?' he said questioningly.

She glanced up and forced herself to meet his eyes. They looked hurt—hurt and confused. She looked away.

'I'm leaving,' she told him quietly.

'Oh, God—because of me?'

Dimly she was aware of Mary and Deborah fading discreetly out of the office.

'I didn't think I could work with you—in the circumstances. I didn't think it would help either of us.'

'But—leaving! Clare, that's—oh, hell. I never meant this to happen.' He sounded genuinely unhappy, and Clare had to quell an absurd impulse to comfort him.

'I'll be OK. I'll go to Cambridge, I think, and stay with my parents for a while. Perhaps I'll get a job at Addenbrookes.'

'I feel as if I've driven you out.'

She stared at him helplessly for a minute. 'Don't

blame yourself. It isn't your fault you don't love
me——'

Her voice broke and she turned away. 'Anyway,
there's nothing to be achieved by discussing it. I leave
at the end of next week.'

He stood behind her in silence for several seconds,
and then he sighed heavily. 'I'm sorry—for what it's
worth. I wish there were some way I could turn back
the clock.'

'That would be too easy,' she said quietly.

'Yes. Perhaps you're right.'

She heard the door open and close behind her, and
sagged against the desk. Only nine more days to go. It
seemed like a life sentence.

Four o'clock came slowly, and Clare gathered her
things and walked through the hospital. She went to
the main entrance to buy a paper from the stand in
Reception, and saw Michael sitting by the main door,
waiting.

She took a deep breath and walked over to him.

'Hi. Do you want me to give you a lift home?'

He looked up and his eyes seemed slightly guarded.

'It's OK, thanks, I've got a lift——'

'Taxi!' a voice hailed cheerfully from the door, and
Clare looked round, a sinking feeling in her heart.

Jo Harding was standing in the doorway.

CHAPTER NINE

SOMEHOW she got through the rest of the week. Michael seemed as happy to avoid her as she was to avoid him, and their contact remained strictly limited to necessary professional exchanges.

She didn't see him with Jo Harding again, but that could have been as much because she avoided all the public places where they might be seen together as because they hadn't been together—however, her hyperactive imagination filled in the missing blanks with Technicolor images that rose up to taunt her in unexpected moments.

She pictured them sailing, swimming, going out for drives, eating cosy little dinners *à deux*, and, worst of all, she pictured them tangled in intimate embraces, and heard him murmuring erotic and tender words of love as he caressed her. She didn't hate him—she couldn't, but she hated Jo, and above all she hated herself for the bitter jealousy which was destroying her memories.

And then on Thursday she found him slumped in Sister's office at six o'clock, his face grey with exhaustion and lined with pain, and all her anger drained away.

'Are you all right?' she asked gently.

He lifted his head and met her eyes steadily. 'I hurt like hell,' he told her wearily. 'My leg aches—both the bit that's there and the bit that isn't—and my back's been giving me stick recently. I think it's because I'm not walking properly yet, and certainly when I stand in Theatre I favour my left leg a lot. Whatever, I hurt like the dickens and I want to crawl into a corner and sleep for a week. I just hope nothing comes up that David can't deal with.'

She smiled sympathetically. 'I can't offer you a corner, but how about a cup of tea before you go home? You look all in. And I can probably find you some supper—we're one patient down on yesterday's bed state, so we'll have a spare meal you could have.'

'Sounds great. Thanks.'

She went out and found the meal, a plate of chicken supreme and rice with fresh vegetables, and took it through to him with a pot of tea and two cups. 'Save me some tea,' she said, 'I've got to go and do the drugs.'

Half an hour later she was back, to find the plate empty, and Michael slouched in the chair, his left leg propped on the desk, fast asleep.

She poured herself a cup of tea and sat watching him. Poor man, he was clearly exhausted. She knew he had rushed his return to work in order to get back in gradually before Tim Mayhew went away, but he was obviously not ready for it yet.

Suddenly his bleep sounded and she snatched it out of his coat pocket and turned it off, reaching for the phone as she did so.

'You bleeped Mr Barrington,' she said quietly.

'Oh, yes, he's wanted in A & E—hold on, I'll put you through.'

Damn, she thought. It seemed a crying shame to wake him. She touched his hand. 'Michael? Wake up, love. You're wanted on the phone—A & E.'

He straightened, blinked and reached for the phone. 'Hello, Barrington here. Can I help?'

She watched his shoulders slump for a second, and then with a Herculean effort he straightened up and took a deep breath. 'Right, I'll come down and see her. Alert ITU in case she needs to go in there, otherwise we have room on the ward—yes, I'm there now, I'll arrange it. Thanks.'

He put down the phone and stood up, wincing slightly as he took the weight on his left leg. 'Young woman with multiple leg injuries. Looks like a possible double amputation. Just what I need. I'll report back when I've seen her. Can you alert my Theatre team? And perhaps you could ring Tim Mayhew at home. I'm not sure I'm up to this—it'll be a long job.'

But Tim Mayhew was in Cambridge at a clinic, and wasn't expected back until after ten.

She greeted Michael with the news when he came up a short time later. His mouth tightened into a grim line and he nodded. 'OK. Get hold of David Blake for me—he can assist.'

'How is she?'

'Bloody awful—shocking mess. Both legs are smashed below the knee, loss of circulation certainly to the right foot and possibly to the left, her chest was compressed by the steering-wheel—apparently a Range Rover went over the top of her car. Tore a wheel off and the only injury the driver sustained was a cut on his head from his mobile phone! I understand he was so drunk they didn't have to use a local to stitch the bastard!'

He was furious. Clare wondered how he'd get through the surgery, in terms of emotional resources.

'Will you be able to save her legs?'

'Or die in the attempt,' he said grimly. 'Get a bed ready for her—I expect she'll go to ITU but she may be stable enough to come straight down here.'

He turned towards the door, and she called him back.

'How about some painkillers? You've got a long night ahead of you.'

He sighed. 'It mightn't be a bad idea. OK, but quick—I need to get up there.'

She handed him four co-proxamol. 'Two for now, two for later.'

'Thanks, Clare.' He stared at her for a second, then, bending forwards, he brushed his lips lightly against hers.

Ten minutes later the phone rang. 'Can you hand over to anyone? My scrub nurse took one look at this lot and keeled over, and I'd like you to assist if you could.'

Clare's heart hammered in her chest. In truth, she hated orthopaedic surgery—all the chiselling and sawing and hammering seemed so barbaric—but needs must, and she had done her stint not so very long ago.

'OK. Deborah Lewis is here—she can give the report to Judith Price. I'll be up in a minute—which theatre?'

'Four.'

'OK. She dropped the phone back on the hook, almost running out of the office to find Deborah. Quickly explaining the situation, she made her way rapidly to the Theatre suite above. An orderly was waiting for her with sterile rubber boots and green trousers and top. She scrubbed and dressed as quickly as she could, and slipped into the theatre beside Michael just as he was ready to begin. David Blake was already busy in A & E applying a plaster, and would join them as soon as possible. Her role, therefore, was even more vital, and she just hoped she was up to it.

Glancing down at the exposed limb, she could see why the scrub nurse had fainted. She looked up and met Michael's eyes over the mask.

'Come over here beside me, Staff,' he instructed. 'I'm tired and I ache. Ignore me if I snap at you, and if you don't understand what I want, ask. OK?'

'Yessir!' She clicked her heels together smartly, and his eyes crinkled.

'Attagirl. Right, let's start with the right leg first, that's the worst. At least it's reasonably clean.' Using tweezers, he picked up a couple of shreds of what could have been tights, and then, using saline solution, he swabbed repeatedly until he was satisfied the area was free of debris.

'Right, now we can see what we're up against. The first thing we have to do is restore circulation to that foot, or she's going to lose it.'

Working rapidly, giving clear and precise requests for instruments, he carefully found and reconnected the mangled arteries and veins. When the tourniquet was released, although some of the minor vessels oozed a bit, there were no major leaks and after a few agonising seconds her foot turned slightly pink.

There was a collective release of breath, and a noticeable easing of tension in the quiet theatre.

'Well done,' Clare murmured quietly, and he gave a soft, rueful laugh under his breath.

'Thanks.'

Amazingly, the nerve damage was minimal, and he was able to repair the small amount of damage with the aid of a microscope.

After one particularly long spell crouched over the instrument, he closed his eyes and straightened with a groan, and Clare signalled to the circulating nurse to find a high stool. She pushed it in behind him, and with a surprised mutter of thanks, he sank back against it and carried on his delicate work.

Having restored the circulation to her right foot to his satisfaction, he then began work on the bones, realigning the shattered fragments with a locking intramedullary nail, and filling in the gaps with chips of cancellous bone taken from higher up her leg. Because of the extensive swelling, he was unable to close the wound completely, instead bringing the sides of the skin together as far as possible and running sutures through fine rubber tubing to give some support to the tissues.

At last he straightened and sighed. 'OK, that's all I can do on this side for now. When the swelling's subsided, I'll close the wound properly and resuture it, probably in a few days, at which time we'll put a cast on to immobilise it more completely—always assuming she hasn't lost it by then. Now, how about the other one—how's she doing at your end, Peter?'

Clare looked up in surprise. The anaesthetist was Peter Graham, the man who had been with them at the time of Michael's accident, and who had assisted at his amputation. She hadn't seen him since, and wondered what he thought of her after her hysteria. Well, at least she wasn't being hysterical now.

He nodded his satisfaction. 'She's doing fine. You've got as long as you need.'

'Thanks.' Michael limped stiffly round to the other side of the table, and Clare followed him. The circulating nurse brought the stool round and positioned it behind him.

He muttered his thanks, hitched it closer with his foot and eased himself on to it with a sigh.

'Bloody leg,' he muttered. 'Right, young lady, what gives on this side?'

They repeated the procedure, this time using a plate and screws to fix the tibial shaft, and realigning the fibula without fixing it.

'I don't want to put any unnecessary hardware in,' he explained. 'She's getting like the Bionic Woman as it is. Right, I think that's all I can do. I'll just close her up and we'll get her into Recovery and start praying. Swab count, please.'

Clare and the theatre nurse checked the swabs and instruments, confirmed the count and Michael closed her leg.

'Excellent—thank you all very much.'

He stood up and stretched, then supervised her removal into Recovery. 'Careful with her as she comes round—remember she's got three fractured ribs that will be giving her hell. I'd better write her up for some pretty substantial pain relief for the first twenty-four hours, I think.'

He turned to Clare. 'I'm going to have a quick shower—will you wait for me?'

'Of course.'

He smiled tiredly and limped into the men's changing-room. Clare made her way to the ladies', and changed back into her uniform, shoving her cap into her pocket. Her feet ached, not surprisingly. She was amazed to discover that it was almost one o'clock in the morning—they had been operating for over five hours. Poor Michael. Her heart went out to him. He must be shattered—he had been tired enough to start with. Gathering her things together, she made her way out into the lobby to wait.

He appeared a few minutes later, his limp exaggerated by tiredness and pain, and the smile he gave her didn't reach his eyes.

'Where are you spending the rest of the night?' she asked him.

'God knows—I hadn't got that far. Why?'

'Come back to my flat. I'll make you a hot drink, shovel some painkillers into you and put you to bed. How does that sound?'

'Fantastic—you have no idea.'

'I think I have—come on, soldier, let's get you home.'

They were halfway down the corridor when they met David Blake coming the other way.

'Better late than never,' Michael said drily.

He laughed tiredly. 'Sorry. I got held up in A & E with another RTA—spinal injury. He didn't make it. How's your patient?'

Michael shrugged. 'It'll be touch and go on the right leg. If she doesn't lose it it's an ideal candidate for non-union—I think the left one will be all right. We'll have to wait and see. I'm going to bed.'

'Lucky you. Well, if you don't need me, I've got another fracture to reduce. See you tomorrow.'

David headed back towards A & E, Michael and Clare towards the residence. She opened the door of her flat and Michael stumbled in behind her, swearing softly under his breath.

'For heaven's sake get the weight off that stump before you damage the thing!' she scolded, and led him through to the bedroom. 'There, take your clothes off and lie down—I'll give you a back massage while the kettle boils.'

She left him for a moment while she put the kettle on, and when she came back he was naked, face down on the quilt, asleep. With the competence of years of practice, she rolled him over, got the quilt out from under him and covered him up. The hot drink and painkillers could wait. What he needed most of all was rest.

She changed and made herself a drink, and sat in the easy chair in front of the television. It was on quietly, to deaden the contrast between the silence of the night and the hushed bustle of a hospital during the grave-yard shift—the ringing phones, the doors banging, hurried footsteps. After the cottage it must seem unbearably noisy. She knew it had to her.

She must have dozed, because she awoke with a start some time later. Michael was muttering, shifting rest-lessly on the bed. She waited for the dream but it didn't come, at least not in its most terrifying form, evidently. After a while he grew quiet again, and then she heard his voice softly in the half-darkness.

'Clare? Are you awake?'

Yes.' She stood up stiffly and went through to the bedroom. 'How are you feeling?'

'Lonely—how about you?' He sounded sad, and very much alone.

'Me, too.'

She knew it was madness—knew she would regret it in the morning, but she had to have one last chance to hold him, to be close to him without rows or jealousy or routine coming between them. Slipping off her robe, she lifted the quilt and slid into the narrow bed beside him.

His arms closed around her and he sighed with satisfaction. 'That's better,' he murmured. 'God, Clare, I've missed you.'

She pressed her lips against his chest and hugged him gently. 'Go back to sleep.'

'Mmm.' Seconds later, his steady, even breathing told her that he had done exactly that.

When the alarm woke her in the morning, he was gone. She jumped out of bed and ran into the sitting-room, but she knew from the quality of the silence that the flat was empty. There was a note propped against the kettle.

'Bless you. Michael.'

She dressed hurriedly, anxious to get up to the ward and see him again. She knew he would be around to see the young woman whose legs he had fought to save, and she wanted to be there. He had been different last night—more approachable. Perhaps now, if they talked, they could unravel the mess they had got themselves in, because she was now quite certain that Ross was right and Michael still loved her. Where Jo Harding fitted in to all this, Clare wasn't sure, but she could even forgive him that if she could have him back. After all, everybody was allowed one mistake, surely?

She arrived on the ward at half-past seven, to find that he had already been to see the young woman, and had gone home to change. Clare was ridiculously disappointed.

Mary O'Brien appeared at a quarter to eight. 'I gather you had high drama last night,' she said immediately. 'I've just seen David Blake—he tells me we've got a young woman with multiple fractures and soft tissue injuries, and that Michael was up half the night trying to save her legs.'

Clare nodded. 'That's right. His scrub nurse passed out and I had to go up and assist—Mary, it was grim.'

'I believe it,' she said with a tight smile. 'Now we have to stand back and let nature take its course. Let's find out how she is.'

They went into the office for the report.

Judith looked up and smiled. 'Morning, Mary—oh, hello, Clare. I wasn't sure if we'd see you today—Michael said you'd been assisting on Sally Pierce till one and might be late.'

'What time was he in?'

'Oh, six—something like that. Wanted to check her circulation.'

'How is it?'

'Good—fine. He was very pleased. I must say, she's a rare mess. I specialled her myself for the first four hours, because I was quite sure she was going to haemorrhage or arrest or something! Anyway, she's settled well. She's still on quarter-hourly obs, and Michael wants Tim Mayhew to have a look at her when he comes round. Apparently he isn't happy with the neurological responses in the right foot, but, as he says, the nerves were damaged so it could take time. Her fiancé's in the day-room, wearing a hole in the carpet, by the way, but she isn't up to visitors yet. Michael said maybe later.'

The rest of the ward had had the usual sort of night—insomnia in the elderly, pain in the post-ops, and Barry Warner had developed a pin track infection in his right leg where the screws of the external fixator penetrated the skin. He was on antibiotics and hourly obs until it stabilised, but it had been caught early on and should respond well to treatment. Apart from that there had been two new admissions who David Blake had been working on while Clare and Michael had been in Theatre.

'Right—I'm off to bed. Haven't had such a busy night for ages! See you tomorrow.'

Sister O'Brien turned to Clare. 'Right, well, as you were in on it from the start, perhaps you could special Sally Pierce for me?'

'Fine.' She made her way to the single room opposite the nursing station where first Michael and then Alan Beedale had been and relieved the staff nurse coming off night duty.

Sally was asleep, her long dark hair lying tangled on the pillow, her face pale except for the vivid bruise over her left eye. She looked extraordinarily young, and very pretty. Clare checked her chart. She was twenty-two. I wonder what she does for a living, Clare thought. She seemed reasonably stable, although her pulse-rate had fluctuated a bit. That could be stress-related, though, depending on whether she had been awake or asleep.

Clare checked the flow of the IVI and the Pethidine pump, and wondered when Michael would be back to see her. Perhaps then——

'Good morning,' he said softly, his eyes crinkling with laughter as she jumped and turned towards him.

'Good morning yourself,' she said with an answering smile. 'You startled me. Are you better?'

'Much, thanks to the TLC. Clare, I think——'

But she never found out what he thought, because there was a quiet moan from the bed, and he stopped talking and bent over the young woman.

'Sally? Sally, you're all right. You're in hospital. Can you open your eyes?'

Her lids flickered up, and she focused slowly.

'How are you feeling? Can you tell me where it hurts?'

'Everywhere,' she whispered. 'My chest hurts, and my legs —my legs are so sore. What happened?'

'You had a car accident. We've done an operation on your legs to line up the bones, but you're doing well now. You've got a few broken ribs, too, but nothing to worry about. OK?'

'Did I break my legs?'

Michael nodded. 'Yes, you did. Don't worry about them now, they'll be fine. I'll give you something to take away the pain, and then try and go back to sleep, all right? You'll feel better later.'

'Can I see Steve?'

'Is that your fiancé?'

She nodded. Michael looked up and met Clare's eyes. 'Is he in the day-room still?'

'I believe so. Shall I go and see?'

'No, I'll have a word with him first. I won't be long.'

Sally turned her head slightly and looked at Clare. 'Do I look OK?' she whispered. 'My make-up must be all over the place——'

'You look fine,' Clare reassured her. Good grief, if she was worried about her make-up, how would she cope when she saw her legs?

A few minutes later Michael returned with a stocky young man.

'Hello, Sal,' he said gruffly. 'How are you?'

'Pretty grim. I must look a fright—I'm sorry. . .'

'Oh, Sal, as if I care about that——' His voice cracked, and he crouched beside her, his jaw working.

She reached for his hand, and he squeezed it gently, pressing it to his lips. 'You must rest and get better, eh? And remember, I love you.'

'Love you, too. . .' she sighed. Her eyes drifted shut, and Steve's head snapped up, his eyes wide with panic.

'She's dead!' he whispered rawly.

'No, she isn't,' Michael assured him. 'She's gone to sleep. I've just increased her pain relief, quite apart from which her system is full of the anaesthetic still, and she'll probably doze on and off for the next twenty-four hours, at least. It's better that she does.'

Tim Mayhew arrived then, and Clare ushered Steve out, promising to keep him in touch.

They turned back the bedclothes and studied the damaged limbs in silence for a second. Then Mr Mayhew raised an eyebrow. 'And I thought you'd worked a miracle with Barry Warner!'

Michael smiled wearily. 'I couldn't give up on her, Tim.'

Mayhew nodded. 'No, I realise that. Well, I think you've done the right thing—her feet are both warm and pink, and neurologically she's got plenty of time for regeneration before we need to worry. No, I think that looks good. Well done.'

He scanned her chart, nodded again and they left the room. Clare did her TPR and BP, and sat down again beside her patient.

It was a long morning. Sally dozed most of the time, and Michael was obviously busy in Outpatients. He popped up again at lunchtime, but Sally was awake and so Clare was unable to talk to him.

She was feeling much more alert, although still in a certain amount of pain, but now she wanted questions answered.

'How bad are my legs?' she asked him.

He pulled up a chair and sat down beside her, taking her hand in his.

'They were very severely injured—not just fractured, but extensive damage to the muscles and blood vessels. It'll be a long, slow road to recovery, I'm afraid.'

Her eyes were wide and serious. 'Will I walk again?' she asked.

Michael hesitated, obviously torn between the whole truth and a palatable dilution. He chose the truth.

'Your right leg is still touch and go. Your left leg is much less badly damaged, and I think it will heal well in time. Provided the right leg stabilises, and the bone knits together, yes, you'll walk again.'

'And if it doesn't?'

'We may have to amputate it below the knee.'

She went quite pale. 'Steve would hate that,' she murmured.

Michael gave a short, bitter laugh. 'Nobody likes it,' he said drily. 'However, it is quite possible to get over it and get on with life.'

His bleep went, and he switched it off and stood up. 'Excuse me, I have to go. I'll be back as soon as I can.'

Clare watched him as he limped down the corridor, and turned back to Sally.

She was staring down the corridor after Michael. 'Has he got an artificial leg?' she whispered, her voice filled with horror.

'Yes. Yes, he has.'

'How dreadful! Was it an accident?'

Clare sat down beside her, in the chair Michael had used, and took her hand.

'Yes, it was an accident—it was six weeks ago today.'

Sally's eyes flew up and met Clare's in astonishment. 'Is that all?'

'Yes. He's really pushed himself, but he's come out on top. We're all very proud of him.'

'Oh, God, I hope it doesn't happen to me—Steve would never get over it. I'd lose him for sure——'

'Not necessarily. There are more important things in a relationship than how many legs you've got, you know.'

She shook her head. 'He always tells me I've got such sexy legs—when he makes love to me—oh, no!'

'Sally, come on, it may not happen. And anyway, if that's all it takes to put him off, he can't really love you.'

She turned back to Clare, her eyes wide with distress. 'That doctor—how did his wife cope?'

'He—he's not married.' She hesitated, unsure how far professionalism could prevent her from giving this young woman the assurance she needed, and then decided her need was greater than Michael's need for privacy.

'We got engaged two weeks before the accident. Everything was wonderful—I'd never been so happy. And then, suddenly, our whole world fell apart. He was so brave—he fought back every inch of the way, and he was up and about in no time.'

'Didn't you hate it—his leg?'

'No, of course not. I hated the accident which had caused it, but nothing could make me hate Michael or anything about him.'

'How did it happen?'

Clare closed her eyes. She still felt chilled when she thought about that day. 'There was a derailment. We had to work in dangerous conditions because the carriages were very unstable. He stayed in a dangerous place because an elderly lady was dying and he wouldn't leave her, and then a gust of wind caught the carriage above and it crashed down and trapped him. It was awful, but it could have been much worse—he could easily have died.'

Sally closed her eyes. 'I wish I'd died.'

'No—you mustn't say that! It isn't true. In a few days you'll feel much better, and by then we'll know if your leg will recover.'

'And if it doesn't?'

Clare squeezed her hand. 'Then you'll be brave, as Michael was brave, and Steve will stand by you, and you'll find that there are more important things in life than being perfect.'

'But he won't want to touch me any more——'

'That isn't necessarily true. It hasn't put me off Michael. On the contrary, his courage and determination have just deepened my feelings for him.'

Sally met her eyes. 'You must love him very much to have stood by him like this.'

'I had no choice—I love him, come hell or high water. He means the world to me, and without him, I'm nothing.'

Sally looked over Clare's shoulder then, and smiled sadly. 'Here he is—you're a lucky man. I wish I could be sure that Steve loved me so much.'

Her heart pounding, Clare turned in the chair and met Michael's eyes. They were guarded, his face a rigid mask.

'Thank you,' he said stiffly. 'Could I have a word, Staff?'

'Of course.' She stood up and walked towards him, unable to meet his eyes.

'In the office—Mary's doing drugs.' He closed the door behind them, and Clare twisted her hands together.

'Michael, I'm sorry—I didn't mean to tell her so much, but she was so afraid——'

'Was it really fair to raise her hopes with those empty promises?' His voice sounded strained.

'What empty promises?' She turned to face him, her heart in her eyes. 'I only told her the truth.'

He stared at her endlessly, as if he was afraid to believe what he could see.

'What time are you off?'

'Four—why?'

'Because I think it's time we talked to each other— really talked. I just hope to God it's not too late.'

She could hardly breathe for the sudden pounding of her heart. 'Too late for what?'

'For us.' His voice was gruff. 'I have to go—I'll see you at the main entrance at four.'

And he was gone, leaving her speechless and trembling in the middle of the office, rooted to the floor.

When her feet came to their senses, she went back to Sally Pierce's room. 'You're looking better—would you like to see Steve if I can find him?'

'Do you think he'll want to see me?'

Clare picked up on the uncertainty in her voice, and hastened to reassure her. 'He was here all night, apparently, asking every passing nurse how you were. He hasn't left the hospital since you were brought in. I would say he wants to see you!'

Sally smiled weakly. 'Perhaps you're right. Yes, I'd love to see him for a little while.'

Clare went up to the day-room and found Steve slumped in a chair, head propped on his hand, fast asleep. She shook him gently awake. 'Steve? Sally's feeling a bit better. She'd like to see you.'

He straightened, flexing his wrist, and tried to smile, then his face crumpled and he buried it in his hands. 'I thought I'd lost her—I thought for sure she'd die. God, if you could have seen the car——' A choked sob escaped him, and Clare perched on the arm of the chair and put her arm around his shoulders.

'Come on—she's going to be all right. Maybe not perfect, but she's very much alive, and just now she's sure you aren't going to want to see her.'

'What?' He lifted his tear-stained face and gazed at Clare incredulously. 'Is the woman nuts? Of course I want to see her. . .'

'Come on, then, or she'll think I'm having to talk you into it. I should go and wash your face and then come down when you're ready.'

He stayed with Sally for half an hour, during which Clare sat outside at the nurses' station to give them some privacy, but near enough to be immediately available should she be needed, and as she listened to the murmured exchanges she prayed that they would come through without all the pain and heartache she and Michael had suffered.

CHAPTER TEN

CLARE wasn't a clock-watcher, but that afternoon she found her eyes straying to her watch with monotonous regularity. The hands seemed to crawl round, and all the time her nerves were winding up tighter and tighter.

Finally it was time to go, and with trembling hands she straightened her hair before making her way down to the main entrance.

Michael was standing by the door waiting, and as she drew nearer she could see the lines of strain etched clearly on his face.

'Hi,' she greeted him, her voice a little taut.

'Hi. I thought we'd go to my place. Are you ready to go?'

She nodded. 'My car's round the side. Do you want me to bring it?'

'No, I'll walk with you.'

'I don't mind—I thought if your leg was still aching——'

'I said I'll walk with you!' he said sharply, and her heart sank. This was never going to work.

They walked in silence round the end of the hospital building to the residence car park, and he got into her car without a word.

The drive to the cottage was accomplished in a tense silence. When they arrived, Michael got out and opened the door of the cottage, and held it for her as she went through.

It smelt slightly musty, as if he was hardly there—which of course, this week, he hadn't been.

They went into the kitchen, and Michael reached for the kettle.

'I'll make a cup of tea,' he said heavily. He sounded defeated, as if even that was too much for him.

'Would you like me to do it?' she offered.

'Stop mothering me! I can cope!' he snapped.

'I'm sorry. . .' She turned away, gripping the back of a chair with her hands until her knuckles were white. Damn it, she wasn't going to cry!

'No, I'm sorry. I didn't mean to shout, it's just that there's so much to say and I don't know where to start——'

'Do you love me?' she said quietly.

'What?'

'You heard.' She turned round to face him. 'Well? Do you?'

'Yes,' he ground out, 'oh, God, yes. I've never stopped loving you.'

'Then why?'

He turned away. 'Because I thought our love too new, too fragile to be asked to stand that sort of test. I had no idea then how much it was going to hurt to send you away from me. I thought, if I went to the boat, it would be easier to forget you.' He sighed. 'I was wrong. It was impossible to forget you. You've been in my thoughts every minute of every hour, every day, since I met you.'

'And yet you doubted my love. You thought it must be pity that kept me with you. You never once asked me outright if I still loved you, and when I told you, you said I was mistaken.'

'I couldn't believe you could love me—not in the same way. Not after what happened.'

'But why? What did I ever say——?'

'In the train,' he rasped, 'when I was going to take off Alan Beedale's foot, you begged me not to. You said he'd be a cripple. I knew how you felt about amputation, you'd made it quite clear the day we met. And then, when we made love, you called me your perfect hero. . .'

He turned towards her, and her heart wept at the anguish she saw in his face. She reached out to touch him. 'Oh, my darling—I've hurt you so much. I never dreamt you'd believe I could be so shallow. Of course I love you. I always will. I never meant to hurt you. . .'

The hot tears spilt down her cheeks, and he lifted his hands and cupped her face. 'Don't cry—no more. There've been enough tears. Come here.'

He wrapped his arms round her and folded her into his chest.

'I love you,' he whispered raggedly.

'I love you, too.'

'Show me—please, if you mean it—show me.'

She stepped back and looked up into his face. It was still racked with doubt, tortured by the spectre of failure. She took his hand and led him slowly up the stairs.

In his room, she released his hand and unbuttoned her dress, laying it carefully over a chair before kicking off her shoes and stripping off the rest of her clothes. Then she turned to him and unbuttoned his shirt, pulling it out of his trousers, throwing it aside and turning her attention to his waistband.

It was slack. 'You're thinner,' she said sadly.

'So are you.'

She slid down the zip and pulled his trousers down, tugging off his right shoe and pushing him gently backwards until he was sitting on the bed. Then she undid the left shoe and pulled it off, and slid his trousers down.

She laid them on the chair with her dress, and then knelt in front of him to undo the strap on his artificial leg.

He flinched, but she gritted her teeth and eased up his leg, removing the prosthesis gently and laying it down beside the bed.

His skin beneath the stump sock was red and sore where the leg had pressed, and she bent and kissed it. 'You've been overdoing it, haven't you? You should rest tomorrow—I think a day in bed should do.'

She looked up at him and smiled through her tears. His eyes were bluer than she had ever seen them, and he reached out his hands and pulled her to her feet.

'Make love to me,' he pleaded, his voice ragged.

'Not yet,' she murmured. 'You need a back-rub. Lie down—and don't go to sleep.'

'Fat chance,' he laughed shakily. He eased aside the quilt and rolled on to his stomach. Clare found the bottle and knelt astride his hips, smoothing the lotion over the warm satin of his back. He groaned as she found the knots and eased and pummelled them out, and as she worked, his tension seeped away until he lay under her hands like a boneless cat.

Then the quality of her movements changed, and she could feel a different tension entering his body at the sensuous slide of her palms over his skin.

'Turn over,' she murmured throatily.

He obeyed, his eyes as they met hers blazing with need.

'You are so beautiful,' she whispered. Then she knelt over him and lowered herself carefully.

He groaned and reached for her, pulling her down into his arms.

'You're a witch!' he breathed, his heart pounding beneath her ear. 'Oh, Clare, I can't hold back.'

'Then don't. There's always next time.'

He began to move, his body urgent beneath her, and suddenly she felt the tension coiling within her, threatening to explode.

'Michael!' she cried, and then the world shattered about her and she collapsed, sobbing, in his arms.

It was a long time before either of them could move. She lay sprawled, half on, half off him, their legs tangled, hands meshed together over his heart.

'Do you believe me now?' she asked him quietly.

'Oh, yes—finally, I believe you. I'm sorry I doubted you. I don't know why I did.'

'Oh, I do,' she said. 'If I'd had a mastectomy I would have found it very hard to imagine you would want me.'

'Clare, that's ridiculous! Of course I'd want you—I'd be sad, dreadfully sad, but there's no way it would affect my love for you, except to make it deeper.'

She twirled the hair on his chest idly with one finger.

'Then why did you find it so hard to believe in me?'

He sighed. 'I think I was just afraid that you might not love me enough. God, I missed you. I was so lonely without you.'

'Was that why you slept with Jo Harding?' she asked quietly.

'What?' He levered himself up on one elbow and

stared down at her, his face puzzled. 'I've never slept with Jo. What are you talking about?'

She closed her eyes. 'Please don't lie to me. I saw and heard you. We were all at that party—last week. I was on the landing looking for Deborah when you and Jo came out of the bedroom. You were all rumpled, and she said, "Better?" and you said it was fantastic, and she said it was a pleasure getting her hands on your gorgeous body—I wanted to scratch her eyes out!'

'Clare, look at me.' She opened her eyes. He looked sad, and very sincere. 'She had just given me a back massage. I told you I'd had trouble with it recently.'

'What about the other times I saw you with her?'

'She's been fantastic—I know she looks like a vamp, but she's got a heart of pure gold. She sat for hour after hour and listened to me while I rambled on about you, and she made me endless cups of coffee and mopped up my tears.'

'Tears?'

'Oh, God, yes—Clare, I was dying without you. There's no way I could have had an affair with anyone else, believe me. She gave me friendship. That's all it was—totally innocent friendship.'

'It didn't seem it,' she said doubtfully.

'It was, I promise. How could you think otherwise?'

'You once said to me that when a beautiful woman throws herself at your feet, it takes a hell of a man to walk away. I didn't blame you. She's very lovely.'

'Oh, Clare. I was trying to put you off me. I thought if I cheapened our love, then you'd hate me. You never threw yourself at me. You gave yourself—and it's a gift I'll always treasure. I didn't mean to hurt you.'

She reached up and touched his cheek. 'I deserved

it. You know I told you Andrew was better in bed than
you? I never slept with him. I was just getting back at
you—I was so angry with you for suggesting we were
having an affair that I wanted to let you think it.'

He laughed and hugged her close. 'It took me all of
forty-eight hours to work that one out. Not even I'm
thick enough to believe that you could do that.'

'You aren't thick.' She kissed him gently. 'Tell me,
why was Pop angry with you?'

'He couldn't believe I was going to break off our
engagement. He said I was doing you a grave injustice,
and if I really thought that you didn't love me, then I
probably didn't deserve you. He said I wasn't to go and
see him again until you were back in my life.' He
laughed. 'I might have known he was right.'

She snuggled closer. 'I'm glad he was. The thought
of my life yawning away ahead of me without you in it
was so awful—thank God I've got you back.' She dug
him in the ribs. 'And in future, if you need a back-rub,
I'll do it!'

He laughed, a low, sexy laugh. 'Oh, promises,
promises.'

Clare sat up and smiled down at him mischievously.
'Tell me,' she purred, 'who's best?'

He laughed. 'Oh, Jo definitely—ouch! No, she does
a pretty mean back-rub, but I must say, you have a
more interesting finish.'

Clare laughed in delight. 'I'm relieved to hear it.'
She lay back down in the warmth of his arms.

'I love you, Michael,' she said quietly. 'Please don't
ever forget it.'

'Never,' he vowed, his voice vibrant with emotion.
'I'll never doubt you again, I promise, and, if it takes
me a lifetime to prove it to you, so be it. Now,' he

rolled away from her and grinned, 'didn't you offer to make the tea?'

'Are you trying to get me out of bed?'

His grin widened. 'You could bring the tray up.'

She smiled. 'How terribly decadent!'

'Mmm.' His eyes gleamed, that missing spark firmly back in place.

'On the other hand,' she said, casually trailing her nails over his chest, 'I could always get the tea later——'

He groaned and reached for her. 'Forget the tea,' he said with a husky laugh. 'I've just had a better idea. . .'

AUGUST 1992 HARDBACK TITLES

SEPTEMBER 1992 HARDBACK TITLES

ROMANCE

Summer's Vintage *Gloria Bevan*	3748	0 263 13279 X
Cry Wolf *Amanda Carpenter*	3749	0 263 13280 3
Ride the Storm *Emma Darcy*	3750	0 263 13281 1
Web of Fate *Helena Dawson*	3751	0 263 13282 X
Love in Torment *Natalie Fox*	3752	0 263 13283 8
Haunting Alliance *Catherine George*	3753	0 263 13284 6
A Woman's Love *Grace Green*	3754	0 263 13285 4
A Daughter's Dilemma *Miranda Lee*	3755	0 263 13286 2
A Bride for the Taking *Sandra Marton*	3756	0 263 13287 0
Private Lives *Carole Mortimer*	3757	0 263 13288 9
Dangerous Dowry *Catherine O'Connor*	3758	0 263 13289 7
Love Like Gold *Valerie Parv*	3759	0 263 13290 0
Stranger Passing By *Lilian Peake*	3760	0 263 13291 9
Prince of Darkness *Kate Proctor*	3761	0 263 13292 7
The Wayward Wife *Sally Wentworth*	3762	0 263 13293 5
Reckless Crusade *Patricia Wilson*	3763	0 263 13294 3

MASQUERADE *Historical*

The Captain's Angel *Marie-Louise Hall*	M295	0 263 13379 6
The Falcon and the Dove *Paula Marshall*	M296	0 263 13380 X

MEDICAL ROMANCE

In Safe Hands *Margaret O'Neill*	D213	0 263 13377 X
Sister at Hillside *Clare Lavenham*	D214	0 263 13378 8

LARGE PRINT

The Golden Mask *Robyn Donald*	551	0 263 13120 3
The Perfect Solution *Catherine George*	552	0 263 13121 1
Spirit of Love *Emma Goldrick*	553	0 263 13122 X
Naturally Loving *Catherine Spencer*	554	0 263 13123 8
A Date with Destiny *Miranda Lee*	555	0 263 13125 4
Reluctant Hostage *Margaret Mayo*	556	0 263 13126 2
The Jilted Bridegroom *Carole Mortimer*	557	0 263 13127 0
Left in Trust *Kay Thorpe*	558	0 263 13128 9

LOOK OUT FOR OUR NEW MEDICAL LARGE PRINT SERIES. THESE ARE THE TITLES FOR JULY – DECEMBER

JULY
AFFAIRS OF THE HEART   Sarah Franklin
THE KEY TO DR LARSEN   Judith Hunte

AUGUST
WINGS OF HEALING   Marion Lennox
YESTERDAY'S MEMORY   Patricia Robertson

SEPTEMBER
DEMPSEY'S DILEMMA   Christine Adams
DOCTOR ON SKYE   Margaret O'Neill

OCTOBER
SAVING DOCTOR
   GREGORY   Caroline Anderson
THE WRONG DIAGNOSIS   Drusilla Douglas

NOVEMBER
THAT SPECIAL JOY   Betty Beaty
A PLACE OF REFUGE   Margaret Holt

DECEMBER
MORE THAN TIME   Caroline Anderson
CLOSER TO A STRANGER   Lilian Darcy